Grinners

Also by G. Kent

Bandits on the Rim

Running with Razors and Soul:
A Handbook for Competitive Runners

Grinners

G. Kent

Bandit Press

ISBN – 13: 978-0615938097
ISBN – 10: 0615938094
LCCN: 2013923517

Bandit Press
2329 NE 8th Place
Ocala, FL 34470
kentib@earthlink.net

This book may be ordered from the publisher, through booksellers, or online at createspace.com or amazon.com.

To Todd and Kerls

of course

Contents

Part One – *The Backpack*

1. Going to Redwood Creek
2. Lebec
3. A Dirty Blonde
4. Deliverance
5. Lodgepole
6. Redwood Creek Trailhead
7. The Lost Trail
8. First Night
9. Rock Slide
10. First Encounter
11. Todd's Surprise
12. The Ranger
13. Louis Disappears
14. Louis
15. Escape
16. My Arrest
17. Sheriff of Merced County

Part Two – *Back Home*

18. My Apartment
19. Thatcher Glass
20. Norm
21. Manny's
22. Sparky
23. Kendall
24. The Phone Call
25. Saugus Railroad Station
26. Canoga Park
27. Back to Manny's
28. County Line Surfing Beach
29. 289 High Performance Mustang
30. Lake Calls Sparky
31. The Team

Part Three – *The Return*

32. On the Road Again
33. A William Golding Novel
34. Military Mindset
35. Return of the Ranger
36. Night Talks
37. Reconnaissance and Ambush
38. Rough Night
39. Kerls
40. Final Ambush
41. The Horror
42. Retreat
43. FBI

Part One

The Backpack

Chapter One

Going to Redwood Creek

When you're crammed inside a pickup truck for over six hours, the conversation has a tendency to go south. Unfortunately, we'd been on the road no more than thirty minutes when Louis began to tell his story.

"On my last camping trip, Ricky Hart brought along a buddy from his insurance office. It was the guy's first backpack and he was a total fuckup."

"I heard this one, Louis."

"Todd hasn't heard it."

"I don't believe it either."

"Which part?"

I tilted my head. "The unbelievable part."

"Shut up, Lake," Todd said. "Let him tell it."

Louis continued. "We camped at Rattlesnake Creek. Not only was the guy a total fuckup, he was a girlie dude."

"Girlie dude?"

"At the creek, I watched him bend over to filter water and he had a nice ass."

"Oh, quit," I said.

"By the third day, it was obvious Ricky and the girlie dude were inseparable. They shared a tent and went on long hikes together alone. They were always grabbing each other's butt in a playful manner. We

1

were all very suspicious and intrigued. The group hatched a plan to unmask what was going on.

"Someone said, 'I think Ricky switched teams.'

"I said, 'No fucking way.'

" 'Then you explain it, Louis.'

"I said, 'Ricky Hart is not gay.'

" 'We're going to need proof.'

" 'What kind of proof?'

" 'Visual proof.'

"I said, 'Nothing I'd want to see.'

"We told Ricky we were going on a hike to the waterfall and would be gone for a couple of hours. We headed up the trail until we were out of sight and then double backed into camp. Someone suggested taking a photo of whatever we found. He said, 'Louis can hang it in the office.'"

I said, "Please stop, Louis."

Todd said, "Let him finish, Lake."

"The camp was empty when we arrived. I figured they were down by the creek. But then we heard moans coming from Ricky's tent. We glanced at one another and smiled. This is going to be ugly, I thought. I unzipped my camera case and nodded. Someone pulled back the tent flap.

" 'Holy crap,' I said, dropping the camera. Ricky Hart and the fuckup girlie dude were naked and doing it."

Todd said, "No shit?"

"Yep. Trying to set the night on fire."

I said, "Who are you...Caligula?"

"Legs and arms were all wrapped around each other."

Todd said, "I feel like I'm in a Russ Meyer film."

"We finally realized the girlie dude was a chick. A very foxy chick, I might add. We had banned females from the camping trip, so Ricky brought his girlfriend and disguised her as a dude."

"You're saying for three days you didn't know the guy was a chick."

"I thought he was kinda pretty," Louis said, "but so are you, Lake."

"Bite me, Louis."

Louis smiled. "I certainly liked Ricky Hart a lot better when everyone thought he was gay."

I said, "Maybe one day when you return to the planet you came from, you'll stop telling that fucking lame story."

Chapter Two

Lebec

We stopped at a gas station with a country market in Lebec, and Todd raced for the bathroom.

I said, "Tell me more about our backpacking site, Louis. Your secret spot."

"Redwood Creek."

"What's so special about Redwood Creek?"

Louis said, "It's a place the National Park Service has lost."

"Lost?"

"Here," he said. "Look at the new map of Kings Canyon. Do you see the Redwood Creek Loop Trail?"

"Clear as day. It's not lost."

He handed me an older map. It was soiled and frayed. "This is a vintage map of Kings Canyon from 1954. Look for yourself."

I carefully unfolded the map and quickly located the Redwood Creek Loop Trail. "Okay, what's so special?"

"Look closer at the map, Lake. Don't be a dumbass."

He was right. I spotted the trail he was talking about immediately. It left the loop trail and headed south on Redwood Creek.

"Hello," I said. "What's this?"

Louis said, "It's a trail that no longer exists. If you are a trail that no longer exists in the backcountry of a national park, you are about as lost as it gets. A ranger informed me that discontinued trails are returned to their natural state. But many of the old trails were marked with orange tin squares nailed to the trees. Though the trail is gone, if we can locate the orange tin squares, we can hike the lost trail."

"Why do we want to go back there?"

"Look at the two tributaries that flow into Redwood Creek. The lost trail leads to a spot that is right in the center of the fork. It's God's country, Lake. No one has camped there for twenty-five years."

I stared at the old map. "You may have a point," I said. "I think I'm getting excited."

Louis nodded enthusiastically. "Game on."

"Why isn't the trail open any longer?"

"It may have been too difficult to maintain or there was bear activity. The point is, we will be alone in the largest redwood forest in the world."

"You think we can find it?"

"You can find it, Lake," he said. "Trailblazing is your forte."

I said, "That's a lot of pressure, but I'll see what I can do."

"Where the fuck is Todd? You ask me to take a dump and I'm back in three minutes."

"Leave him alone."

"Let's see what he's doing."

"I know what he's doing."

5

"C'mon."

"He's not like us, Louis," I said. "He's a decent guy and won't appreciate the humor."

Louis nodded. "Then let's teach him a lesson."

In the first stall of the bathroom, I saw Todd's hiking boots. So did Louis. He glanced at me and beamed.

No, I said, without speaking.

"Hey, motherfucker," Louis shouted, banging on the stall. "No shitting allowed in here."

There was total silence. Louis was smirking. A solid, muscular Chicano opened the stall door. He glared at Louis and then turned his attention to me.

"You assholes want to 'splain yourselves?" he demanded.

"Jesus," Louis stuttered. "I…"

I said, "Big mistake, man."

"Huge," Louis added.

"*Lo siento, amigo.*"

Suddenly the Chicano got a crazed look on his face and I thought he might take a swing at me.

Louis held up a hand. "Whoa, dude," he said. "Think about it. We're real sorry about banging on the stall door, but there's still only one of you and two of us."

I clenched both fists and waited.

The Chicano narrowed the slits in his eyes, cocked his head and then left the bathroom.

Todd strolled out of the second stall with a huge grin. "Hope you bastards learned a lesson."

Louis said, "That dude would have been a handful."

I nodded.

Chapter Three

A Dirty Blonde

Beer was a necessity for the afternoon drive, so Todd and I sauntered toward the country market. Louis sat in the truck and guarded the gear. The market's dusty windows were adorned with a dozen neon signs advertising beer and cigarettes, very cheap beer and cigarettes.

A longhaired teenager with metal stud earrings and bloodshot eyes hung out near the entrance.

"Hey, buddy," he said, "you look cool."

"What do you want?" I asked.

"If I give you some money will you grab me two quarts of Jim Beam?"

"Why would I do that?"

He pointed. "See what's standing next to the van?"

I looked. Three girls, who were maybe fifteen and practically naked, leaned against the van door and waved.

"So?"

"So...we can take those babes for a drive up Lebec Canyon and party. You in?"

Todd was snickering.

I held up my hand. "Please, dude. Give me some respect."

The punk gave me the finger and stomped off. We entered the market and looked around. Stacks of cases and twelve-packs were everywhere.

I said, "There's more beer on the floor than in the freezers."

Todd peered down an aisle. "Beer sales must be pretty brisk in Lebec."

I carried a twelve-pack of iced Budweiser to the counter. The girl working the register was a dirty blonde and pretty, but looked as though she had been rode hard and put up wet. She observed what I was buying and then gave me a knowing smile.

"Damn," she said. "It's only eight in the morning."

"So what?"

"Fucking Budweiser for breakfast," she hooted. "My best girlfriend drinks fucking Budweiser for breakfast. She's a piece of work."

I said, "You realize I may be drinking it later."

"Not my fucking girlfriend."

"Maybe you should introduce us."

"She'd be a load of trouble, but you're welcome to try." She looked Todd and me up and down. "Damn. You guys look like some of them Woodstock hippies."

Todd said, "We just left Woodstock a few days ago. Jimi Hendrix blew my mind."

She cocked her head. There was something not quite right about her teeth, but I was sure she'd be an accomplished fuck. She dropped some of my change on

9

the floor and bent over. Her ass was perfection. Todd and I smiled at each other.

She looked up. "Woodstock, huh? Oh, bullshit. You guys get out of here and don't come back unless you mean business."

Todd said, "Is that an invitation, darling?"

She licked her index finger. "Only if you mean business."

As we left the market, I said, "Don't say a word. We're going to Kings Canyon."

"But if her friend looks as good as her, we gotta go back."

"You're married, asshole."

"In name only."

Chapter Four

Deliverance

Todd opened the truck door and said to Louis, "I think *Deliverance* was filmed in this town."

"Possibly."

I said, "*Deliverance* is a masterpiece. It would have won best picture if it weren't up against *The Godfather*."

"Scared the hell out of me."

Todd said, "It was Burt Reynolds's finest performance. He was a young Marlon Brando. If he had continued to land roles that showcased his acting skills rather than wasting his talents in those moronic *Bandit* films, he could have been a De Niro or Pacino."

Louis said, "I liked him in *White Lightning*."

"*Deliverance* was Jon Voight's movie," I said. "The scene on the cliff was awesome."

"Ronny Cox was the film's conscience."

I said, "He was good, but his character was a wuss."

Todd said, "Did you know James Dickey played the sheriff?"

I tilted my head. "Really?"

"He nailed that part."

Louis shook his head. "Neither of you recognize the true genius in *Deliverance*. Ned Beatty delivered the finest performance of the decade. I felt far more sympathy for him than Ronny Cox."

"Ronny Cox's character was killed."

"So?"

I smiled. "You may have a point."

Louis said, "Imagine playing a male rape victim. What if the scene had more than one take? Uh, Mr. Beatty, sir, I'm sorry but we need a different angle for the buttfucking scene, and do you think you could squeal with a little more enthusiasm?"

"I have a favorite line in the movie," I said. "As they start to bury the hillbilly, Ronny Cox's character says, 'We can't do this. It's against the law,' and Burt Reynolds scans the forest and then shouts, 'The law? What law, Drew? Show me the law.'"

Chapter Five

Lodgepole

In the late afternoon, following a brisk swim at the Marble Fork of the Kaweah River, we pulled into Lodgepole Campground in Sequoia National Park. As we set up camp, we checked out one another's food and equipment.

"Todd has a new North Face tent," Louis observed.

"You still have the nicest pack," I said.

Louis smiled with satisfaction. "Vintage L. L. Bean."

Todd said, "Check out Lake's new REI sleeping pad."

We argued over who had the coolest knife. Our Coleman stoves, water filters and mess kits were state of the art, but food was still the primary source of pride.

Todd said, "I brought a mini cooler." It was the size of a shoebox. "I have enough cheese, butter and Snickers for everyone."

"I ground French roast coffee."

"I made Gorp," I said. Louis and Todd nodded respectively. There's no set way to make Gorp, just about any mixture will work, but my recipe was famous. I took pride in the variety. Peanuts, cashews, raisins and sunflower seeds formed the base, while Cajun sesame sticks and jalapeno almonds added spice.

Dried cranberries, dark chocolate bits and M&M's were the surprise.

Louis lived on beef sticks and jerky. Once he included cans of tuna and boasted his dinner was surf and turf. Other than that, four days in the woods meant rice, noodles, oatmeal and Pop-Tarts.

Louis said, "I even brought popcorn."

At that moment, a ranger walked into camp with that annoyingly officious look. "You can't have three tents on a tent pad," he said, getting right to the point.

"Excuse me?" I said.

"It causes overuse. Park regulations state that tent pads can only accommodate two tents."

Louis said, "These are only backpacking tents. They don't take up half the pad."

"One of you has to move to a different site."

"And pay another fee?"

"Yep."

"You can't be serious."

"Seventy-five dollar citation serious."

I said, "We have one lousy truck and three tiny tents. The campsite across the road has three trucks, two giant tents hanging off the pad and eleven people. And you say we're causing overuse?"

"You have five minutes before I write the ticket."

"Have some compassion, dude."

"Five minutes."

Louis said, "I really like that big buckle on your hat. Without it you might look really stupid."

The ranger's face turned red. "What did you say?"

"I wanted to be a ranger," I said, "until I found out one of the requirements was my parents couldn't be married."

"You want me to toss your ass outta here, wise guy?" he snapped.

"You'll lose a camping fee."

"Five minutes."

After he left, Louis said, "I'll move my tent. I can't believe they let those dickweeds carry guns."

I said, "I'm walking to the store. Need anything?"

Todd said, "I'll go with you."

At the park store, in the back of the freezer, I found a four-pack of Olde English 800 for a dollar ninety-nine. It was the foulest tasting yet most lethal malt liquor on the planet.

"Want one?" I asked Todd.

"Absolutely not."

"I'm going to buy a can for Louis and me."

At the counter, the teenage cashier with a nose ring and blank stare rang it up. "A dollar ninety-nine," she said.

I tilted my head. "But it's a dollar ninety-nine for the four-pack."

"So?"

"So I'm only buying two."

She checked a list next to the register. "It says Olde English 800 singles are ninety-four cents plus tax."

"That makes no sense."

"Why not?"

I became exasperated. "So I can go back and get the other two from the four-pack for free?"

She thought long and hard about that one. "I guess."

"Jesus Christ," I muttered, grabbing the other two cans.

Two old rubes sat on a bench in front of the camp store. One said, "If it don't give you a headache, it ain't no good."

The other nodded.

The first old rube was whittling on a piece of wood. As I passed by, he looked at me and dropped the piece of wood at my feet. I picked it up and something sharp cut my finger.

"Ouch," I said. The old rube grinned.

I glanced at the carving. It was the face of a pretty young girl with large eyes and curly bangs. The craftsmanship was excellent. Then I noticed a fiendish smile with long sharp teeth. I had cut my finger on a tooth. The smile was totally disturbing.

"Better get a bandage on that finger, pardner," the old rube said.

"You bet, pop."

I handed back the carving.

"Thanks, pardner," he said. "See you real soon."

When we were out of earshot, I said, "What was that all about?"

"Moonshine," Todd said. "When it hits your brain, you feel achingly good."

"No, I mean the old dude's carving."

"I didn't see it."

I shivered. "It was a girl with a hellish grin. She looked like a demon."

When we returned to our campsite, Louis was happy about the Olde English. "Two of these will give you a mean buzz."

I said, "Speaking of buzzes, what is everyone drinking in the wilderness? I have a quart of Jack Daniel's."

"Quart of Johnny Walker Black for me," Louis said.

Todd said, "I brought two bottles of chardonnay."

Louis shook his head. "Hold onto a tree…we're gonna get shit-faced."

Chapter Six

Redwood Creek Trailhead

Upon entering Kings Canyon National Park, we hit a fork in the road. One way led to Grant's Grove and the other to Fresno.

"Which way?"

Louis said, "We missed it."

"How could we miss it?"

"I don't know, but Redwood Creek turnoff is before this fork."

"Marvelous."

Louis said, "Ask the old dude sitting in front of that cabin."

I crossed the road and turned onto a gravel driveway. I said, "Good morning, sir."

Before I could say another word, the old dude pointed with his crooked finger back down the road we had come and said, "Four miles back on the right is the turnoff to Redwood Creek."

"Thanks," I said and then re-crossed the road. "Either he's a mind reader or gets asked that question a lot."

Louis and Todd nodded.

It was a twelve-mile drive down a bumpy dirt road to Redwood Creek trailhead. Todd didn't handle the bumps very well.

He said, "I never did take that dump after you banged on the stall door."

Louis smiled at me and said, "Told you it would work."

Todd was sitting in the middle of the truck cab. When I parked at the trailhead, he scrambled over me and stepped on my groin. Louis and I watched him sprint to the Andy Gump.

"I won't shit in those things," I said. "I overheard a guy complain to his wife that when his shit hit the bottom, a large gob splashed up and struck him in the ass."

"Jesus, Lake. You say my stories are gross."

At the trailhead, we rechecked our packs. Two chunky girls, with short hair and muscles, hiked out of the woods and flopped down their packs next to ours.

I said, "How was it back there?"

The chunkier one said, "Cosmic. It was totally cosmic."

"Get much rain?"

"Lord, son," she said, indignantly. "You got to expect rain in the Sierras."

The other one noticed Louis was wearing his Tarzana Boxing Club tee shirt and said, "I wouldn't go back there, tough guy."

"Why not?" Louis said.

"You think you're tough?"

"Tough enough."

She smiled sweetly. "Don't say I didn't waaarrn you."

The two girls slung on their packs and hiked toward the road.

"What was that all about?" Todd asked.

"Did you hear her warn me not to go back there?"

"I heard." Todd said. "I would have punched her, but I was afraid she might take me down."

"Lord, son," I mimicked. "You got to expect rain in the Sierras."

Louis said, "Those girls are scary."

"What do you mean?"

"Did you see their knives?"

Todd said, "You're joking."

"No, they have big fucking knives on their belts."

"They're backpackers," I said. "Of course they're carrying knives."

Louis said, "Then explain the blood on their shirts."

"Blood?" Todd said.

"The one I spoke to had deep scratches on her arm," I said. "They must have tromped through a briar patch."

There was only one other vehicle in the parking lot. It was a beat-up National Park maintenance truck.

I said, "Let me see your map, Louis." He carefully unfolded the vintage 1954 Kings Canyon map and handed it to me.

He said, "We hike five miles on the loop, and as soon as we cross Redwood Creek, we fan out and find the lost trail."

"I wonder where the chunky girls camped," I said.

Chapter Seven

The Lost Trail

The five-mile hike on the Redwood Creek Loop Trail was not difficult and it traversed some of the most beautiful country on the planet. Nothing compares to the splendor of a mature redwood forest, and Redwood Creek compared favorably to the Giant Forest in Sequoia and Rockefeller Grove in Humboldt. Redwood Creek differed from the other groves in one crucial respect: with the exception of the bloody, knife-wielding chunks – no people.

Early on the loop, we took a wrong fork and came to a dead end. Todd had fallen back. Louis and I stared at each other.

"Damn."

Louis said, "Todd ain't gonna like this."

"I don't like it."

"Here he comes."

Todd waved when he saw us, and then his shoulders drooped when he realized our predicament. "No, don't tell me."

"Just shut up and turn around," Louis said.

We made it to the bridge in two hours. The creek was wide and swift, and the redwood groves were at their thickest.

Louis said, "Fan out. This may take some effort. According to the map, the lost trail is on the east side of the bridge."

"You realize the trail hasn't been maintained for twenty-five years," Todd said. "These woods could swallow an interstate in twenty-five years."

"That's why I brought Lake. He's our Daniel Boone."

For the next hour, I was meticulous. I took ten to fifteen yard swaths from the creek and methodically bushwhacked sixty to seventy yards into the forest. It was slow and difficult trailblazing, and after an hour I had found no trace of the trail.

Louis and Todd began to scout for an alternate route along the creek. Just when I was about to join them, I spotted a faded orange tin square nailed to a tree. I pushed through the brush for a closer inspection. It was definitely an old trail marker. I stared into the forest and squinted. After a moment or two, I saw another orange tin square about thirty yards away. In between the markers were thickets, fallen logs and baby redwoods. The trail was indeed gone, but the tin markers had survived.

I shouted, "Here she is."

We crashed into the wilderness and found the third marker. Then we stopped and scanned the horizon. Louis said, "See anything?"

"No."

"There," Todd said, and we marched on.

It was painfully slow going. Several times we plunged forward and hoped for the best. Someone always kept an eye on the current marker, which was our temporary home base. It would have been impossible to follow the trail alone or at night. What should have been an easy forty-five minute stroll turned into a three-hour ordeal. It was nearly dark.

I saw it first. At the bottom of a hill was a flat clearing that straddled Redwood Creek and was flanked by its two tributaries. A lip on the creek formed a twin waterfall.

"Eureka," I said. "We have arrived."

Both sides of the creek had a sandy beach. A rickety bridge was still in place over the water.

"Un-fucking-believable," Todd said.

"Better set up camp," Louis advised. "Thirty minutes to blackout."

Chapter Eight

First Night

The tents went up quickly. Amid plenty of jokes regarding our blowing techniques, the air mattresses took a little longer. Stoves and water filters were placed in a circle around the proposed campfire. No fire rings had survived the twenty-five years.

As we combed the brush for wood, Todd proved himself to be the expert. He crawled under boulders by the creek and found primo dried logs. Louis and I nicknamed him Gatherer of Wood.

The flat was remarkably cleared, though no signs of a campsite remained. It was a circular meadow about fifteen feet above the creek. Three separate redwood groves formed a perimeter. The last orange tin square led down to the rickety bridge. Todd and I would have nothing to do with it, but Louis carefully picked his way across to the other side and reported no more markers. The twin waterfalls were almost annoyingly loud.

Before Happy Hour began, I crawled into my tent and placed my flashlight and toiletries within reach. I also unzipped the case to my Smith and Wesson snub-nosed thirty-eight. I held the piece in my hand and clicked open the cylinder. Five bullets were loaded with five more in the case. I didn't tell Louis or Todd about my piece because both disdained firearms.

Down at the sandy beach on our side of the creek was a large boulder with a ledge wide enough to set up our snacks and booze. We loaded it up. Beef sticks, cheese, crackers and Gorp were spaced between Jack Daniel's, Johnny Walker Black and a bottle of chardonnay.

Louis said, "If other backpackers walked into camp, I'd pretend not to know Todd."

"I even brought a plastic wine glass."

"You could also order a skirt and two tickets to *Boys in the Band*."

"Shut up, both of you," I said. "It's Happy Hour."

We proceeded to snack and get pleasantly intoxicated. For dinner we cooked a pot of rice with slices of beef sticks and jerky over an open flame. Louis swore meat tasted better cooked over an open flame than on a Coleman stove. But the open flame blackened the bottom of the pan and caused a layer of rice to be caked and crusted.

Todd said, "If Sparky served this rice for dinner, our divorce would be final." He then took out his knife and scraped the bottom in order to eat the burned portion.

While washing our dishes in the stream, the current swept away my brand new pan. "Goddamn it," I said.

Louis and Todd snorted with laughter.

"Go ahead, you donkeys," I said. "Laugh it up."

We turned in early, each to his tiny nylon bedroom. I stripped down to my boxers and slipped into my sleeping bag. When the fire finally died, I closed my eyes and dozed off. My REI sleeping pad was decadently luxurious.

My eyes opened and I had no idea where I was. The sound of the twin waterfalls leaped at me from the blackness. The night was claustrophobic. I climbed out of the tent to take a leak.

This place is spooky, I thought, as I zipped up the flap.

Just when there was a faint grayness in the east, Todd let out a yelp. My heart raced as I slapped the ground searching for my thirty-eight.

"Todd," I hissed. "What is it?"

He said, "I thought there was a bear in my tent."

I relaxed. "Go back to sleep."

"Hey, Lake."

"What?"

"This place is spooky."

Chapter Nine

Rock Slide

Early on our first morning, I went to the creek to read and get away from my friends. I found a sweet spot with frothy white water and a sandy beach. I could lie in the sun all morning without fear of intrusion. Then I heard a shout. I climbed up on a boulder and, sure enough, here came Louis and Todd marching along my exact route.

"Like bloodhounds," I said.

They disappeared behind a clump of dogwoods with Louis in the lead. Picking out a decent sized rock, I hurled it in front of Louis to startle him.

"Ouch," Todd cried. Somehow he had switched places with Louis and taken the lead. Inadvertently, I smacked him in the chest.

"Damn it, Louis," Todd said. "Who threw the rock?"

Louis made a face of mock disbelief. "Gee, Todd, I don't know. Who could have thrown the rock? Let's see, I'm here, you're here…where's Lake?"

Todd frowned. "Sarcastic bastard."

"Dumbass."

"Sorry," I called from behind my boulder.

Louis said, "Come with us, Lake. I want to show you what I found while looking for wood."

Todd said, "I'm going to have a bruise."

I shrugged, sheepishly.

We came around a bend in the creek and Louis said, "Check it out."

There was a perfect twenty to twenty-five foot rockslide on one of the tributaries feeding Redwood Creek. At the bottom was a four-foot pool.

"Nice," Todd said.

"Let's do it."

I wagged my finger and said, "Don't you dare."

Louis said, "Excuse me?"

"Don't slide down that rock."

"Grow some balls, Lake."

Todd said, "What's your problem?"

"The granite could rip your ass off. Look at those rocks and submerged logs in the pool. If you hit your leg, it will fracture. Once you push off, there's no stopping until you hit the water."

Louis said, "Thanks for the advice, Mom. Me and Todd are sliding."

"Maybe Lake is right."

"No, Lake suffers from wussism."

"Have you forgotten about ethics, Louis?"

"What ethics?"

"The backcountry ethics that say 'never do something stupid unless it's absolutely necessary.' If you get hurt, how am I going to haul your ass back to the trailhead? When you're in the wilderness, it's your responsibility not to get hurt."

Todd said, "He's right, Louis."

"I know he's right, damn it. John Fucking Muir. Let's do it anyway."

"Roger that," Todd said.

Chapter Ten

First Encounter

While Louis and Todd were playing on the slide, I explored farther down creek. The day was sparkling and delicious. Redwood Creek was a wilderness deep in the heart of Kings Canyon National Park, and bushwhacking off the established trails took the experience to a higher dimension. The desolation was indescribable; it transcended words and deciphering. The massive redwoods huddled in groves and poked holes in the sky.

My trek down creek was not difficult. I was forced to wade several times, but that only made it more fun and interesting. A large flat rock sat in the middle of the creek and created an irresistible island. After dunking in the water, I climbed on the rock and let my drippings cool the surface.

This was going to be my afternoon sanctuary. I brought with me Edward Abbey's *Desert Solitaire* and a flask of whiskey.

After about an hour a tall, pretty brunette slipped out of the woods and crouched next to the creek. She looked up at me.

I said, "Hey."

"Hey yourself."

"Like to share my whiskey?"

She waded halfway to my rock. "Maybe."

31

"You startled me," I said.

"Really?"

"We're a tad off the beaten path."

"Where are you camping?" she asked.

"At a clearing about a half mile above the rock slide."

She smiled coyly. She was wearing an incredibly tiny red two-piece. On a log, however, she had set down what appeared to be a black gown.

"Come join me," I said.

"I better not."

"C'mon," I urged. "I promise I don't have fangs."

She giggled. "I have chores to do."

"Chores?"

She nodded. "Visit me tonight at our camp."

"What camp?"

"I'm camping with my sister and some friends."

"I'd like that."

"It's a date," she said. Then she grinned. But not a normal grin. Her grin was an enormous contorted leer. It took up half her face and obliterated her prettiness. I was unnerved.

"Bring your two friends," she added.

My heart skipped a beat. "How do you know about my two friends?"

"We've been watching you," she said. "I think my sister will like them."

I looked at her with my mouth open.

"Our camp is up there," she said, pointing to the woods and continuing to grin. "See you tonight."

Back at camp, after I told Louis and Todd about my encounter with the grinning girl, they both scoffed.

Louis said, "You're so full of shit."

"What are you trying to pull, Lake?"

"Nothing."

"Give me a fucking break. There are no girls out here."

Todd said, "You're trying to spook us."

"No, I'm not."

"I've been down that creek twice," Louis said. "I didn't see a pretty brunette. I didn't see another camp. I didn't see shit."

I said, "She was a fox."

"I'm sure she was."

"But what was with that grin?"

"You're an idiot," Louis said. "A foxy girl invites you to her camp and grins, and you freak out."

"It was more than a grin. It was disturbing."

Louis said, "Enough, Lake. Now you're spooking me. You made the whole thing up."

"Why would I do that?"

Todd said, "You're a writer."

"So?"

"You're writing a spook story with us as the main characters."

Louis said, "This reminds me of something that happened with Ricky Hart. We were hiking up a box canyon near Sedona. It was July and the heat was murderous. There was not one car at the trailhead. Near the end of the four-mile trail, we stopped to smoke a joint. Just as I lit up, Ricky said, 'Shit, here comes someone.' I doused the joint. But when I looked up the trail no one was there. 'It was a nice-looking brunette in red shorts,' Ricky said. 'She's gone now.' We continued up the trail and it dead-ended under a large overhang with a five hundred foot drop. There was no way out except the trail. I never did see the pretty brunette in red shorts."

"What are you saying?" Todd said.

"She was a ghost," Louis said. "Maybe Lake's brunette with a grin was a ghost too."

"Lake, you better not be fooling around."

"I'm not."

Todd shook his head. "You're both spooking me."

Chapter Eleven

Todd's Surprise

A few hours later, Louis said, "Show me where you saw the girl."

"What for?"

"Maybe we can sniff out her camp."

"Want to go, Todd?"

"No way," he said. "I'll hold down the fort."

Louis and I took off. We had just waded across the creek and climbed to the top of the flat rock, when suddenly a loud crashing noise propelled its way through the woods directly toward us. I braced for a band of demons.

It was Todd.

"You're not going to believe what just fucking happened," he said.

"Tell us," I said. I was alarmed by his language and tone.

"I was in the hammock reading my book and a dozen birds started to chirp. The chirping seemed so choreographed, I'm certain it was actually people making the sounds. Then a young blonde appeared at the edge of the redwoods and boldly strutted into camp."

I was aghast. "She walked into our camp?"

" 'Hello,' I said. 'Where'd you come from?'

" 'Surprise,' she exclaimed. She stopped at the fire ring. 'Come with me.'

" 'I'm waiting for my two friends,' I answered.

" 'Please,' she said, and held out her hand. 'We can have fun.'

"I said, 'I can't right now.'

"She motioned with a finger for me to follow and continued her march through camp. Then her smile spread out into a grotesque grin. It was as exactly as Lake had described: disturbing and satanic. She entered the forest on the other side of camp and vanished. The birds stopped chirping and I decided to find you guys."

"You are fucking with me," Louis roared.

Todd said, "She wasn't a brunette so that means there's more than one."

I said, "Girls like that always have dudes."

"Someone else was making those bird noises."

Louis said, "This is starting to annoy me."

Todd glanced toward the shore of the creek and said, "I say we pack up and get the hell out of here."

"What for?" Louis asked.

"Something weird is happening."

Louis said, "It's too late. The hike would be treacherous in the dark."

I said, "I'm willing to try."

"It would be foolish, Lake. Let's hunker down tonight and keep our wits."

"People are fucking with us, Louis."

"We can hike out in the morning."

I said, "Why do you want to stay so badly?"

"Excuse me?"

"Todd and I are scared shitless, and you have a smirk on your face."

"For one thing, I haven't seen a grinning girl. Plus, you're talking about two girls. I figure we can beat the shit out of two girls."

Todd said, "Might be trouble if there were three."

"Bite me, Todd."

"My girl said she'd see me tonight."

"Jesus, Lake," Louis said. "Stop freaking out."

I said, "You're the one who brought us up here with all that lost trail talk."

"So what?"

"Tell me the truth, Louis. Are you setting us up? Is this one of your infamous pranks?"

"Lake," Louis protested. "I'm on edge too."

"I remember in high school when you brought me out to an abandoned house up Old San Fernando Road and had Ricky Hart and another guy inside with candles and Halloween masks. You scared the shit out of me."

"But I couldn't even find the trail. You did. I could suspect you and Todd are playing a prank on me."

Todd said, "Yeah, that's real likely."

"I swear. I'm not playing a prank."

"Fine," I said. "I guess we're stuck here tonight."

Louis said, "Nothing happened last night. Let's build a bonfire and stay up late."

I said, "I didn't want to tell you, but I brought my thirty-eight. If any of your friends are out there, you'd better call them off. If I get scared, I'll shoot at shadows."

"Fuck you, Lake. I told you it's not me."

It was quiet and tense for a moment.

Todd said, "There is something we haven't thought of."

"What's that?"

"What if we're all victims of a prank? What if these other backpackers are out here playing a game or trying to frighten us off?"

"That's gotta be it, Lake," Louis said excitedly. "Did you recognize those girls? You both know most of my friends."

I said, "Motherfucker. What was that old maintenance truck at the trailhead?"

"Didn't even look like a forest service vehicle."

Louis said, "Tonight we stay close. We can sleep outside our tents."

"Tomorrow we get the hell out."

Louis said, "Tomorrow we kick some ass."

Chapter Twelve

The Ranger

Just about the time we were ready to hunker down in our sleeping bags, a ranger wandered into camp on horseback.

"Hello to camp," he said. "I'm coming in."

We stared at him, incredulous.

"A little late to make a house call," Louis said, after the ranger settled down next to the fire.

"I've had a long day," he said. "Covered nearly twenty miles."

I continued to stare in disbelief. "What are you doing out here? You're not even on a trail."

"Might ask you the same question."

"Is that your truck at the trailhead?"

He hesitated. "Nope."

Louis got up and went to his pack. He unfolded the vintage 1954 trail map. "I want to show you something," he said. "See this trail? It's not on any of the park's new maps. We followed it by tracking the faded orange tin squares nailed to the trees. Figured we'd be alone out here."

The ranger said, "Shouldn't hike up closed trails. There's usually a good reason why they're closed."

"Such as?"

"Bear or mountain lion activity, flash flood zone or unstable redwoods."

Todd said, "Why is this trail closed?"

"Damned if I know. It was before my time."

I said, "I got a question."

"Ask it."

"Why are you patrolling a closed, non-maintained trail?"

"They have me collecting water samples," he said. "Something is wrong with the salamander population down stream."

"We've seen other – "

"Todd," Louis snapped.

The ranger said, "Other what?"

"People," I said.

"Backpackers?"

"Perhaps."

"Could you be more specific?"

Todd said, "We don't know who they are. We didn't see any camp or equipment."

"What did you see?"

"Two pretty girls on separate occasions."

"Two pretty girls back here?"

"Yep."

The ranger chuckled. "Call yourselves lucky."

I said, "I'm not too sure about that."

"Why not?"

"It's difficult to explain."

"Really?" the ranger said. "Let me take a guess. Were they grinning?"

I was floored. "How did you know? Did you see them?"

He shook his head. "No, but there's an old park legend in Kings Canyon."

"What legend?"

"Grinners."

Louis said, "What's a grinner?"

"One explanation involves families who refused to give up their homesteads when Kings Canyon was designated a National Park in 1929. Many of them were grandfathered in so they could live out their natural lives on their property. The legend claims descendents of the holdouts also refused to leave and still roam the backcountry today tending to family graveyards and other legacies."

"What about the grins?"

"The grins were supposedly developed as a way to scare off trespassers. I've heard it's a ghoulish display and will frighten the hell out of a backpacker."

Louis said, "Bullshit. You're making this stuff up."

"Well, I've never seen a grinner. You apparently have."

Louis pointed at Todd and me. "No, they have."

"I've also never seen the first hint of a hidden camp."

Todd said, "The girl I saw was not a product of some in-bred hillbillies. She seemed quite modern and at ease."

I said, "What's the other explanation?"

41

"I was afraid you'd ask," the ranger said. "You won't like what I have to say."

"Say it anyway."

"Members of the Manson Family."

"What?"

"The Charles Manson Family had hundreds of members. Six were arrested. Rumor has it the leftover members moved to Santa Cruz and briefly turned the town into the 'Murder Capital of the World.' There were reports of headless bodies found in abandoned cabins and strewn along the seashore. Then the members drifted up here. It's suspected the woods are an operational command post and initiation site where they anoint new recruits and brainwash them with Family philosophy."

Louis said, "This is too bizarre."

"Since 1975 scores of backpackers have reported seeing grinners. Two months ago, a backcountry ranger discovered a system of trenches and underground bunkers that were recently abandoned in the Muir Grove area."

Todd said, "Are we in danger?"

"I've no idea," the ranger said. "I doubt it, but…"

"But?"

"There are stories."

I said, "You remind me of the YMCA counselors who scare the hell out of the little campers just before lights out."

He said, "Keep your eyes open. There's a healthy bear population out here. Remember, you are not supposed to be back here and I could write up a citation. But you seem like nice boys."

"Thanks," Louis said. "We ran into a grouchy ranger at Lodgepole."

He smiled. "Rangers who don't range have a tendency to become assholes." He mounted his horse and started back in the direction he had come. "Adios."

"That was weird," I said. "I don't believe there are salamanders in the park."

Todd said, "He looked exactly like the actor Keith Carradine."

"That motherfucker could be part of the prank," Louis said. "He's probably laughing it up right now with his fellow rangers. It's a game they play to stop illegal camping."

Todd said, "If that's his game, it's working."

Chapter Thirteen

Louis Disappears

Next morning Todd and I demanded to pull out. Louis insisted on nosing around.

I said, "Don't go back to the flat rock. I have a bad feeling about that place."

"I won't. I want to track down Todd's girl. It's daylight now. I want to find out what's happening."

I zipped up my pack. "Please, Louis," I begged. "Don't go."

"Anybody want to come along?"

"Fuck no!" Todd said with emphasis.

I said, "Please, Louis."

Louis looked at his watch. "I'll be back by 10:30."

By noon he had not returned. Todd and I were packed and ready to go.

Todd said, "What do we do?"

"We can't leave him."

"I know we can't leave him. I asked what do we do?"

I sighed. "Fuck if I know. We wait."

"Do you want to look for him?"

"Do you?"

"No," Todd said. "He knows we're waiting. I think we should just stay put."

"Maybe I can find him."

"We need to stick together, Lake. It's not smart to separate."

"Then we wait."

The afternoon dragged. Todd and I didn't talk much nor did we leave the camp perimeter. We were both agitated. The creek and redwood forest remained magnificent and indifferent. Our mental state was quickly deteriorating.

It was Happy Hour and still no Louis.

Todd said, "I don't have any more chardonnay. Two bottles for two nights."

"There's one bit of good news."

"Bite me, Lake."

I said, "I still have some Jack Daniel's, and I know where Louis keeps his Johnny Walker Black."

"It's not like Louis to miss Happy Hour."

"I am aware, Todd. No need to mention it."

"Sorry."

Louis missed dinner too. Thank goodness Todd and I were nearly drunk. In desperation, we went into Louis' pack and finished off his Johnny Walker.

Todd said, "I hope he gets pissed about his scotch."

"This is un-fucking-believable."

"Should we set up the tents?"

I said, "I'm sleeping next to the fire."

It was total darkness. "I'm sleeping next to you."

I looked at Todd. "Do you think he's playing us?"

"Do you?"

"I don't know. He's always been a prankster. I can imagine him out there with Ricky Hart and a few others laughing their asses off at our predicament."

"I don't think so, Lake."

"How can you be sure?"

"I can't. Is that what you believe?"

"It's a possibility."

"But do you believe it?"

I looked into the fire. "No. I've got a feeling about this place and it's not very pleasant."

Chapter Fourteen

Louis

That night I suffered from a horrifying nightmare. A girl's voice whispered, "Don't say I didn't waaarrn you." I climbed to the top of a fallen redwood log and pulled the sleeping bag over my head.

Louis was standing in a small clearing less than half a mile from our camp. He had found the remnants of a recent campfire. The trees began to rustle and then shake violently. Twigs flew out of the woods and struck him on the back.

"Lake?" he said. "Is that you?"

There was a moment of calm. Birds began to chirp. The forest remained aloof and noncommittal. Louis knelt by the fire and sifted through the ash. He felt warm embers.

"This is odd," he said.

Twelve grinners attacked simultaneously from twelve different directions. They wore black-hooded gowns and brandished long knives. Twelve blades twisted in twelve parts of his body. Blood streamed from his wounds as he fought to keep his eyes open. He saw twelve terrifying grins and then blackness.

Chapter Fifteen

Escape

At first light, Todd and I broke camp. The day was fresh and sparkling. The twin waterfalls cascaded into the pool and made their usual roar. Everything seemed to be in its natural place.

I said, "We're going to have to fan out to find Louis."

"No way, Lake," Todd said emphatically. "You and me ain't separating."

I looked at the ground. "You're right."

"If we don't find him by this afternoon, we've got to hike out and get help."

"We'll find him," I said. "He can't be far off."

"Then why hasn't he come back? He's been gone for nearly twenty-four hours."

"He could have twisted an ankle. More likely, he's lost. It could happen to anyone out here away from the creek and off the trails. He's probably waiting for us to find him."

Todd shook his head. "No way Louis would just sit down and wait for us. He'd crawl if he had to. Why isn't he yelling his head off?"

I bit my lip. "He's got to be somewhere."

We began to prepare for a search. Ten minutes later, I was down at the creek refilling the water bottles with my filter.

Todd shouted, "Louis is back."

I looked. On a nearby hill with a few small redwoods, Louis was leaning up against a tree.

"Thank God," I called out, but then my tremendous relief was quickly replaced with anger. "You bastard, Louis. You scared the shit out of us."

Todd yelled, "Where've you been?" He dropped his pack and started to walk toward the hill.

"Wait," I said, putting a hand on his arm. "Something moved behind that tree."

"What?" Todd asked, his voice cracking.

Louis was limp and blood-spattered. Black-gloved hands tied him to the tree with rope. His head sagged.

"He's faking," Todd said. "That's Ricky Hart behind the tree."

Todd and I hesitated. Louis stared at us with blank eyes. I said, "Don't move. This isn't right."

"No shit!"

I yelled, "Is this a prank, Louis? It's not very funny."

"Come down here, Louis," Todd demanded.

Louis did not move. "He's fucking with us," I said.

"I'm not so sure, Lake. What should we do?"

A girl emerged from behind the tree. She wore gloves and a black-hooded gown. She was also grinning, maniacally.

Todd cried, "Holy fuck!"

"Hold your ground."

Two bearded males appeared dressed in similar fashion. Several more grinners stepped out of the woods. I counted at least fifteen, and they were all flashing large knives and grinning. Standing at the end of the line, I recognized the two chunky girls from the trailhead. One of them winked at me. Those fucking bitches, I thought.

"Show 'em your knife, Todd," I said, getting an adrenaline surge.

"They can't kill us," he said. "It's against the law."

I scanned the perimeter and said, "The law? What law, Todd? Show me the law."

I grabbed the thirty-eight from my pack and hid it behind my back. In the other hand, I held my knife.

There was a short intermission. I said, "Slowly back up to the first orange tin square."

"What about our stuff?"

"Leave it."

An elderly man with a long serrated knife stepped to the front of the group. I stared at him closely, and then gasped. It was the old rube from the Lodgepole camp store. He tossed something in the air and it landed at my feet. I glanced on the ground and saw that it was the carving of the pretty girl with a demonic grin. Motherfucker! When I looked up, the old rube was grinning. I shuddered.

"Howdy pardner," he said. "Remember me?"

"What do you want?" I cried.

"I finished my whittling," he said. "I'm going to bury it with you."

I said to Todd, "We're gonna have to make a run for it."

"Lead the way."

"You stay on my heels."

At that moment the grinners charged. They swarmed down the hill, waving their knives and grinning.

"Let's go," I screamed.

The attack was swift and ferocious. Todd and I raced between the trees, but then I tripped over some vines and Todd tumbled over me. Almost immediately, two grinners caught up and sliced at us with their knives. Razor sharp blades cut into my arm and shoulder. Todd let out a groan. We started to run again. I looked back and saw the old rube right on my heels. I was shocked he could run so fast.

I pointed my thirty-eight and said, "Pardner this."

The gunshot sounded like an explosion. It seemed to surprise the other grinners. My bullet tore through the old rube's skull and he went down in a splat of blood. I stopped running and fired two more times, definitely tagging another grinner. Todd took the lead. The grinners had vanished behind the trees.

"Where are they?" Todd asked, gulping for air.

I said, "Keep running."

Suddenly, at least ten grinners flanked us on the right side of the next orange tin square. I fired once more, blindly. Todd was dragged to the ground. I kept running.

Just before I reached the main loop trail, I heard a shrill cry followed by several bird chirps. I stopped and aimed my gun. It began to sprinkle and I could hear thunder in the distance. I waited. Three, five and then ten grinners appeared. The pursuit had stopped. I continued to point my thirty-eight but did not shoot. The rain came down harder. The lead grinner waved, and then they disappeared.

On the loop, I calculated it was about five miles to my truck. I was determined to run the entire distance. I checked the cylinder on my gun and saw there was only one live round left. A loud crash sounded in the woods. I snapped the cylinder shut and fired wildly. A mule deer bounded into the brush.

I said, "Shit, shit, shit."

Chapter Sixteen

My Arrest

Just when I thought I couldn't run another step, I stumbled into four backpackers marching down the trail. The looks on their faces told me I wasn't a pretty sight. Disheveled and soaked with blood, they must have thought I was an escapee from an insane asylum.

"Don't go back there," I warned. "There are killers. My two friends…" I whirled around, but there were no grinners in pursuit. "Don't go back there," I repeated.

I started to run, and they got out of my way. It felt much safer having them between the grinners and me. They watched my retreat and then conferred. After a moment, they decided to continue on.

By noon I reached my truck and realized the key was in my pack. The only vehicle in the lot was the beat-up park maintenance truck. After several frustrating moments, I located my emergency magnetic key under my pickup's back bumper.

At the turnoff to Redwood Creek, the intersection was buzzing with park rangers and Merced County sheriffs.

"I apologize, sir," the ranger said at the checkpoint. "We're investigating reports of gunshots in the area. I'm sure you are aware firearms are prohibited in Kings Canyon National Park." Then he saw the dried blood from the knife wounds on my neck and shirt. He backed up and pointed a finger at me. "Sir," he shouted. "Show me your hands and get out of the truck."

I said, "It was me. I fired the shots."

A deputy said, "Then you are under arrest."

"Officer," I said. "I had just cause."

"You can explain it to the sheriff."

He placed my hands behind my back and fitted the handcuffs.

Chapter Seventeen

Sheriff of Merced County

I spent most of the afternoon receiving forty-seven stitches to my arm, neck and shoulder. The next morning, a deputy brought me from my cell to the sheriff's office.

I said, "Why didn't I see the sheriff last night?"

The deputy didn't look at me. "He was doing investigative work."

"About the murders?"

"About you."

"Me?"

I walked into the sheriff's office and told him everything, even about me shooting the old rube. I left nothing out. He listened patiently, but had the look of someone who was having his leg pulled and knew it.

"I'd like to believe you, son," he said, emphasizing the word 'like.' "We've heard stories of strange sightings in that park, but nothing like this. You seem sincere."

"It's all true," I said, my eyes watering. "I swear."

"We'll be going out to Redwood Creek this morning to have a look-see. I'm waiting on my deputies to bring out the ATVs. How are your wounds today?"

I ignored the question. "Sheriff, I believe my two friends, Louis and Todd, were murdered."

He said, "Mr. Lake. There has not been one confirmed murder in the entire history of Kings Canyon National Park. I don't know if you're lying or the victim of an elaborate hoax. If your friends are out there, we'll find them. If we find them, I guaran-damn-tee they'll be okay. You wait in the outside office until my deputies return."

With the ATVs we made the five-mile loop to the bridge in thirty minutes. I rode behind the sheriff. None of the lawmen were very thrilled when I pointed to the first orange tin square.

"You hiked through that shit?" the sheriff asked, incredulous. "How far?"

"Maybe two miles. It's hard to judge."

"With backpacks? Son of a bitch."

A deputy said, "You boys searching for Sasquatch?"

The other deputy said, "Growing dope, I suspect."

I frowned. "We wanted to follow the lost trail."

The second deputy said, "You're a liar."

"My two friends may be dead."

"I doubt it," he said with a sneer.

"Shut up, both of you," the sheriff barked. Turning to me, he said, "Lead us to your campsite."

I was terrified hiking back to our camp. Though the officers were armed, there were only three of them. If I had killed or wounded two grinners, there would be at least thirteen to fifteen left. I was certain there were more.

56

The deputies acted cocky and unconcerned, as did the sheriff. My problem was they had confiscated my thirty-eight and did not return it.

When we reached the campsite, I went into momentary shock.

The sheriff asked, "Why are we stopping?"

I said, "This is it."

"This is what?"

"This is where we camped."

"Here?"

"Yeah."

He looked around. "I thought you said you left your gear."

"I did."

"Where was your fire?"

I checked the ground and pointed. "Right there."

The first deputy knelt down and stirred up the dirt with a stick. "No fire here," he said.

"Maybe it was over there."

The other deputy said, "No one has camped here for years."

Indeed, the site was clean and natural.

I said, "I don't understand. I woke up right here yesterday morning. The grinners must have cleaned up the site."

The first deputy tossed his stick and said, "You're a goddamn liar."

"Fuck you," I said.

"Lake," the sheriff snapped. "I've got some questions for you back at my office."

"Aren't we going to search for Louis and Todd?"

"We'll poke around a bit for your friends."

The hike back to the bridge was completed in silence. The two deputies snickered at me and pretended to wipe away tears. One offered a hanky. At the station, the sheriff led me to his office.

He said, "Let me ask you one question, Lake. If you were me, what would you think?"

"I swear it's all true. I swear to God."

"I made some phone calls last night and discovered some interesting facts about your buddies, Louis and Todd."

"Like what?"

"Like Todd is in the middle of a nasty divorce."

"Divorce, maybe," I said. "Not too nasty."

"Louis recently lost his job at Paine Webber. He also carries some serious credit card debt caused by some reckless poker playing in Vegas."

I said, "I know about the poker debt. That's the first time I heard about him losing his job at Paine Webber."

He said, "Let me give it to you straight. This looks like a setup."

"No."

"What's your game?" the sheriff asked. "Did Louis and Todd run off to escape a gambling debt and alimony? Did they leave you to explain everything with this ridiculous story about grinners? If I were you, I'd be pissed."

"Even if what you say is true, don't you think we could have come up with something better than grinners? Besides, Todd's wife makes more money than him. There wouldn't be any alimony."

"I think you heard about the old grinners legend and took advantage of the situation."

"Why would I go along with it?"

"You're best friends. The three of you are old college roommates at San Fernando Valley State. Plus, you hope to grab some headlines."

"Excuse me?"

"I know you're a foreman at Thatcher Glass, but it's also common knowledge that you're an aspiring writer. You even published a few spook stories in the magazine *Black Mask*. If an editor believed this grinner nonsense, it might be your big break."

"Look," I said. "I've told you the truth about what happened at Redwood Creek. I'm sure Louis is dead. I don't know what happened to Todd."

"You just ran off and left your best friend."

"I told you fifteen grinners were chasing us. I ran for my life."

"See, that's another thing I don't believe. How did you outrun fifteen grinners?"

"I don't know," I admitted. "My thirty-eight helped. How do you explain my knife wounds?"

"Self-inflicted."

"Don't be asinine."

"Lake, you need to understand. I'm a good friend with the *Fresno Bee* editor. He's not going to publish any accounts of this grinner bullshit. It would cause a panic. The national park might have to shut down. If you go to the *L. A. Times,* we will make you look foolish."

I said, "I swear I'm not looking for any headlines. My friends are missing and could be dead. You need to take that seriously."

"They'll turn up," he said, smiling. "I'm sure of that."

I hung my head and didn't answer.

"Go home, Lake," he said. "Go home and don't come back. Don't you ever try to pull a stunt like this again."

He handed me my truck key and thirty-eight. Pointing toward the door, he said, "Go home."

A reporter from the *Fresno Bee* was waiting outside.

"May I ask you some questions?" he asked.

"I know one thing," I said. "Your sheriff is going to lie to you."

"You can tell me the truth."

"What do you know about grinners?"

His face blanched. "I've heard rumors."

"That's your story."

Part Two

Back Home

Chapter Eighteen

My Apartment

I sat on a leather couch in my tiny apartment on Nordoff and Sepulveda and stared at the phone. It was Sunday evening and my lights were dimmed. I arrived home late Saturday night and had not left the apartment.

The building was seedy and dilapidated. My apartment was upstairs in a far corner with a fine view of the back alley. It was a one bedroom with a small living room, breakfast nook and kitchen. I dressed it up with fresh paint, cheap antique furniture and a New Mexican theme. The two most distinct aspects of the apartment were its high ceilings and vintage hardwood floors.

Sometime in the near future, I was going to have to call Todd's wife, Sparky. Then there would be a face-to-face with Louis' father, Norm. I dreaded both conversations. I didn't know Sparky too well, but Norm had been my Little League coach and cross country trainer at Monroe High School. He had been my only father figure as a teenager.

I noticed blood seeping through my bandages and took another pain pill.

Louis and Todd were dead; I was certain of it. Why had I survived? On the morning of the attack, I had been so scared I wasn't sure if I would ever get over it or feel safe again. My loaded thirty-eight sat on the couch. When the sheriff of Merced County said, 'You just ran off and left your best friend,' it made me feel like crap. On top of that, I had to go to work in the morning. The *L.A. Times* had run a small article about the alleged disappearances. There were pictures of Louis and Todd. A reporter had called but I refused to speak to him. At work, I was going to be inundated with questions.

The phone rang and I nearly hit the ceiling. It was Sparky. I let out a loud sigh and said, "I'm so sorry about what happened, but I'm too messed up to talk now. I'll come by this week to answer all your questions. I promise."

"Just tell me where he's hiding, Lake," she said.

"He's not hiding anywhere, Sparky."

It was quiet on the other end of the line. I could hear her breathing. Sparky was a professor of environmental science at San Fernando Valley State College in Northridge and a tough girl. She clearly didn't believe me.

She said, "I've been doing research for two days and found out that there have been nine confirmed disappearances in Kings Canyon over the past six months."

I raised my head. "What?"

"Nine other confirmed disappearances."

I exploded. "That fucking Merced sheriff claimed there'd never been a suspicious incident in the park. He accused us of engineering a hoax and then kicked me out of his office."

"Some cases have been attributed to runaways, but the nine confirmed disappearances are unsolved and very suspicious, especially the case of two college girls from Tucson. One of their fathers is a state senator."

"I'm going to call that asshole sheriff tonight."

Sparky said, "Please, Lake."

I knew what she wanted and gave her a brief description of the assault. "I don't really know what happened to him. I heard him groan, and then he went down." My voice trembled. "I kept running."

"What else could you have done?"

I thought about it. "I could have stayed with him and died."

"Don't be absurd."

"I'll come by Wednesday after work."

I was determined to call that lying sheriff. Fortunately, I got hold of a deputy who had been off duty Friday and Saturday. He was oddly sympathetic. He assured me it would be his ass if the sheriff found out who gave me his telephone number. I swore an oath of secrecy.

The old bastard was pretty cranky when he answered the phone. "How the hell did you get my number?"

"You gave it to me," I lied. "Don't you remember?"

"What do you want, Lake?"

"Why didn't you tell me about the other disappearances? Why did you and your deputies work so hard to make me feel foolish?"

"Calm down," he said. "Those other cases involve runaways. Two of those youngsters later showed up back home."

"Why didn't you mention the nine confirmed disappearances?"

"I don't like your tone, Lake."

"My tone?"

"You're out of line."

"What about the college girls from Tucson?"

"How'd you get that information?"

I continued to lie. "I spoke to a *Fresno Bee* reporter outside of your office and he was very helpful."

"The Tucson case is being handled by the FBI," he said. "They haven't told me jack-shit. The park rangers worry if the case receives too much publicity it will cause a panic and they'll have to close the park."

"What about my case?"

"Don't come back here, Lake," he warned. "Let me handle it."

"Handle what? You said you didn't believe me. Your deputies called me a liar."

"Maybe I was a little hard on you."

"What am I supposed to do, sheriff? I'm dying over this."

"What you don't want to do is come back here," he said, forcefully. "I'm warning you, Lake."

I hung up and called Norm.

Chapter Nineteen

Thatcher Glass

I had worked at Thatcher Glass in Saugus since college. Two days after graduating from San Fernando Valley State, I took a job for $3.10 an hour on the factory line. I wanted to work with my hands and not have to think about it after I got home. I was fortunate. In three years, I had worked my way up to lead man and then foreman.

My factory built boxes to ship the glass. We made boxes in all shapes and sizes to fit the orders. My major duties were to supervise the packing of the glass into the boxes and to frame out the semi trailers or freight cars to keep the glass from jiggling. The box factory worked around the clock with day, swing and graveyard shifts. Each shift had two supervisors, four foremen, eight lead men and one hundred and twenty workers. I was on day shift.

My supervisor and best friend was Bud. He was a burly ex-con Cherokee, who could kick everyone's ass at the factory. He had taken me under his wing and become my mentor.

Just before first break, Bud pulled me outside next to the lumber pallets and said, "What the hell happened, Lake?"

"Some real bad shit happened, Bud. I'm positive Louis and Todd were murdered." I told him the whole story. "I shot this old dude right in the face."

"Newspaper didn't mention anything about grinners. Authorities claimed your two buddies ran off because of personal issues."

"It's all lies. Louis and Todd aren't coming home and the sheriff of Merced County is trying to make it look like I'm pulling some sort of a hoax."

"Are you pulling a hoax, Lake? I've got to be honest, it all looks very suspicious."

"I swear to you, Bud. The sheriff is hiding the facts about nine other disappearances."

"Honest Injun? You know I take that as a sacred oath."

"Honest Injun."

"I'm going to believe you because you swore it to my face, but don't forget that I know Louis. He's a major league smart ass. Don't take it personal if I seem skeptical."

"Why would I lie?"

"The *Times* article hinted you might be writing another horror story for *Black Mask*."

"No," I said. "I couldn't write about my two friends being murdered."

A couple of forklifts arrived with a load of lumber. The lead man was Kerls. After dropping his load, he jumped off the lift and ran to the lumber pallets.

"Holy shit, Lake," he said. "Are you okay? I heard you got stabbed."

"Several times." I lifted my shirt and showed them my forty-seven stitches.

"What happened to your buddies?"

I said, "It sure didn't go down the way the *L.A. Times* reported."

"How did it go down?"

"Let's meet after work," I said. "I'll tell you all about it."

Bud said, "Manny's?"

"I have to meet with Louis' dad first," I said. "I'll be at Manny's around 9:00 p.m."

They nodded.

Chapter Twenty

Norm

"Welcome, Lake," he said at the front door. "Come in."

"Norm," I stammered. "Sorry I'm late." We stepped into the living room. A small lamp lit the room. "Where's Sally?"

"In the bedroom. It's not that she doesn't want to see you, Lake. She's having a difficult time with all this."

"I understand."

Not only had I been through Little League and high school cross country with Norm, he had also hired me to work in the summers at his pest control business in Burbank. Louis and I had been quite a team doing spray jobs and rodent control. He was practically my father too. Louis got his brains from Sally, but his looks from Norm. He was tough and rugged. He had seen more than his share of combat in the Korean War. As a hobby, he raced Shelby Mustangs.

"Sit down," he said. "Beer?"

I nodded and glanced around the dimly lit room. There were photos and trophies from baseball and cross country. Norm watched me look at the pictures.

He said, "Those were good days. You boys were athletes and real fun to watch."

A tear slid down my cheek. "I don't know what to say. I'm so sorry."

"What really happened, Lake?"

I told him about the two girls and their grins. I said, "It was unnerving. Todd and I wanted to leave in the morning, but Louis insisted on tracking down the grinning girls. He promised to be back in two hours."

"Why didn't you go with him?"

I hung my head. "I fucked up, Norm. I never thought he'd find the girls, and I certainly didn't think his life was in danger. They were just girls."

Norm brought our beers from the kitchen. "You never saw him again?"

I looked up. "Yeah, I saw him. What did that lying sheriff tell you?"

"He said Louis vanished."

I said, "The next morning Louis appeared on a hill. His body was limp and blood spattered. Black gloved hands tied him to a tree. I can't be certain he was dead. At the very least, he was injured and unconscious."

"Then what?"

"Then twelve to fifteen people dressed in black hooded gowns came out of the forest and glared at us. They were brandishing long knives and grinning. Todd and I pulled our own knives and I reached for my thirty-eight. When we began to retreat, they charged."

"Are you making this up, Lake? Are you covering for Louis and Todd? You wouldn't do that to me, would you?"

"I swear, Norm. It's all true. I wish I was pulling a prank."

"You know about the poker debts?"

"Yeah, but not the actual figures."

"Sixty-three thousand dollars. Did you know he lost his job?"

"Not until the sheriff told me."

"Was Todd getting a divorce?"

"I don't know…maybe."

"The sheriff thinks it's an elaborate hoax to escape the debt and alimony, and he may have a point. He claimed they found no evidence of a campsite or struggle."

I said, "That's true, but Louis did not run off. I wish he had, but he didn't unless…"

"Unless what?"

"Unless Louis and Todd played a prank on me."

"A prank sounds like Louis and you know it."

"If that's the case, I still shot an old dude in the face. The sheriff made me feel like shit with his accusations, but he failed to mention there are nine unsolved disappearances in the same general area over the past six months, including the case of two college girls from Tucson. One girl's father is a state senator."

"How do you know that?"

"Sparky told me. She did some research. The sheriff conceded the disappearances when I called him last night. He claimed the FBI is handling the Tucson case."

Norm said, "I'm going to call that jack wagon in the morning."

I nodded. "Give him my warmest fuck you."

Chapter Twenty-One

Manny's

South of Roscoe near an overpass on Sepulveda was Manny's bar. Despite the raunchy neighborhood of cheap liquor stores, fleabag motels and neon-lit strip joints, Manny's was a surprisingly elegant establishment. It had soft lighting and luxurious leather booths.

Manny's Coors Original draft was the coldest in the Valley. Bud sprinkled salt and Tabasco sauce into his beer.

We huddled in a cozy corner booth with a clear view of the traffic on Sepulveda and the Dodger game on KTTV. Dusty Baker had just slammed a solo homerun against the hated Giants.

Bud said, "If this were just you and Louis, I'd be very suspicious. But I can't figure the Todd factor. Todd's a schoolteacher and wouldn't involve himself in any of Louis' shenanigans."

I said, "Everything I told you is true, Bud. I'm not this good of an actor."

"Today's article in the *Times* brought up Todd's divorce. You told me yourself he wanted to break it off and move to Oregon."

"Then why didn't he just move to Oregon? Why all the drama?"

"I don't know," Bud admitted. "To make a clean break, I suppose."

"That makes no sense."

"You're right. That's why I can't figure it."

Kerls said, "Louis has serious money issues. He couldn't move to Oregon quietly. The debt would follow him."

I said, "I know it looks suspicious, but I was there. It happened. The second *Times* article said I arrived home safely, but didn't mention the attack or my wounds. I showed you how I was carved up."

"Let me lay it out for you, Lake," Kerls said. "Louis escapes a huge credit card debt, Todd gets a clean start, and this grinner crap gives you one hell of a scary story."

I looked out the window. There was a hard rain in the street. "Let's order another pitcher."

"Are you playing us, Lake?"

"Fuck you, Kerls."

"If I'm going to help you, I need to know I'm not going to be just another chump character in your next spook story."

"I just told my oldest friend's father that his son is dead. Do you really think I could pull shit like that on a man who is like my own father just so Louis could get out of paying back a little money and Todd can make a clean start?"

"Significant money."

Bud said, "Give it a break, Kerls. We pushed him like we agreed and I believe him."

Kerls nodded. "Okay."

I said, "I know people aren't going to believe my story, but it's true. I'm scared to death and can hardly sleep at night."

Kerls said, "Bud and I are here to help."

"Great, but how?"

"Let's go back to Redwood Creek."

I tilted my head. "Are you out of your fucking mind?"

"We can get to the bottom of this," Kerls said.

"Did you not hear me? There are grinning lunatics out there with big knives."

Kerls said, "We'll go back in a group. This time we'll know what to expect. We pack major firepower and maybe capture a grinner."

I said, "I'm not going back."

"I'm talking semiautomatic rifles. I know some dudes with sick military experience."

I looked at Bud. "Would you go back to Redwood Creek?"

"I would if you asked me."

Kerls said, "Think about it, Lake. It might be better to face your demons."

"And get my throat slit."

Chapter Twenty-Two

Sparky

The next morning Sparky called at 5:30 a.m. I said, "Let me wake up. I told you I'd come by on Wednesday."

"I'm in the phone booth at the 7-Eleven."

I sighed. "Then come up. Bring some coffee."

My upstairs apartment was way in the back. It had a superb view of the alley and dumpsters.

Sparky sat on the leather couch. "Your place is much nicer than I imagined."

I blinked twice. "Which planet are you from?"

She said, "It's not cluttered or messy. New paint, simple furniture and gorgeous wood floors. I like it."

"It's small. What did you expect? Mattresses on the floor?"

"You're an enigma, Lake."

I studied her closely. She was tall, athletic and had long black hair.

"This is the worst of times," I said.

She put a hand on my arm. "Listen to me, Lake. I want you to do me a favor."

"Sure."

"Also, I want you to know the problems Todd and I have been experiencing are…" She struggled with the words.

"Are?"

"My fault, not his. We have tiny problems. I don't want a divorce."

"Does he know that?"

"We haven't had much time to talk. Our major issue is the college wants me to evaluate water quality in rural Guatemala. It's an excellent career opportunity, but I would be gone for three months. Todd was upset when I agreed without discussing it with him. On Friday, I found out I could do the study during the summer months and Todd could come with me. It would be like an extended second honeymoon. Now he's gone and I can't tell him the good news."

"I'm so sorry."

She said, "I want that favor now, Lake."

"Okay."

"Tell me where he is. Please."

"I already told you, Sparky."

"I don't believe you. Your story is wrong. It has Louis written all over it."

"No."

"Stop it, Lake."

I shook my head. "I'd give my life to tell you it's a hoax and he's moved to Oregon. When he went down, I kept running and didn't look back. I'm so ashamed. Now no one believes me, not even you."

"It's too ridiculous. Grinners? You're a writer. Couldn't you come up with something better?"

"My two best friends are probably dead. I can't come up with anything worse."

She began to sob. "I need to talk to him, Lake."

I clenched my teeth. "He did not run off."

She said, "I talked to the Merced County sheriff last night. He insists it's a missing person case. He also says you're full of shit."

"He's covering his ass."

"Why?"

"Because he's not doing a thing about our case."

"He says there is no case."

"What about the missing Tucson girls?"

"He claims they're unrelated."

"Last night at Manny's bar, two of my co-workers suggested we go back to Redwood Creek with some heavy artillery and capture a grinner."

Sparky perked up. "Take me."

I shook my head. "It's not going to happen. You don't know what it's like back there."

"If you go back, I want to go. You know I can tough it."

A chill raced down my spine. "I'm too scared to go back."

Chapter Twenty-Three

Kendall

A few years ago there was a film called *Klute*, starring Jane Fonda. For those who are familiar with that movie, you know my girlfriend Kendall. She's twenty-five and divorced, and the moment you lay eyes on her you want to have sex. She's tall and slender with nice curves, and her big brown eyes are so dark they're almost black. Her teeth and mouth are perfectly shaped, and she talks in that quick, halting Jane Fonda manner. She's smart, with little formal education, and works as a hospital aide hoping to become a nurse.

Kendall sat down on my leather couch and asked, "Do you want to stay here tonight?"

"I do."

"That's cool. We haven't been together for two weeks."

I looked at her long legs. "Since the backpacking trip, I want to stay here every night."

"Jesus, Lake. You are spooked."

"I feel better when you're with me."

"Are you still taking me to the party this weekend in Canoga Park?"

I looked her over again. She had shoulder-length jet-black hair with curly bangs and gypsy earrings. There were several bracelets on each wrist, and two choker chains adorned her neck. She wore a tight black t-shirt and low-cut jeans that exposed her bellybutton. I'd take her to the North Pole this weekend if she asked.

"Yeah, sure."

She said, "I know you're down, Lake, but I need to ask you a question."

"Ask it."

"Don't hate me."

"I know the question, Kendall. It's already been asked many times by friends and the law."

Her eyes opened wider. "It's true, isn't it? It really happened."

"Yeah, it did. Not only do I have to live with the fact that I ran while my friend was being hacked to death by grinning maniacs, I also have to put up with no one believing me."

"I believe you."

"I also have a queasy feeling."

"Why?"

"I see their grins when I close my eyes," I said. "This isn't over. Something dreadful is going to happen."

"Why do you say that?"

"I killed one of their leaders."

"You think they might come to the Valley?"

There had been a third article in the *L.A. Times*. My arrest mug shot was included. In the article, a *Fresno Bee* reporter finally brought up the rumor about grinners.

"At least they spelled my name right," I said.

Kendall opened her purse. "I have some pills. Wash a couple down with some Jack Daniel's and you'll forget about the grinners until morning."

"Thanks." I knocked back the pills with a shot of Jack.

"Guess you don't want to watch *Fright Night with Elvira*."

"What's the flick?"

"*Night of the Living Dead*."

"Not much grinning in that movie," I observed. "I can always watch Elvira."

Kendall said, "Come here. Sit next to me."

I sat down on the leather couch. She smelled delicious.

"Kerls and Bud want me to go back to Redwood Creek."

"Go back? Why?"

"To capture a grinner."

"Don't you dare."

"I don't want to but…"

"But what?"

"It may be best to face my demons."

She slouched back and pulled me closer. "No more talking," she said, pressing her lips against mine.

Chapter Twenty-Four

The Phone Call

Something unexpected happened after Kendall left. My phone rang and it was the sympathetic deputy who had given me the sheriff's home phone number.

"I am totally fucked if anyone finds out I told you this shit," he said.

"I'd never tell."

"You probably have more right to know than anyone else."

"Is this about the Tucson girls?"

"No, I'm not going to tell you about them or any other pending case. It's about the new rumors flying about in Kings Canyon."

"New rumors?"

"Though the official line is to deny, many rangers are convinced that grinners are terrorizing the park. A lot of shit has happened. Backpackers have reported strange sightings for years. Cars of the missing have been recovered at remote trailheads, but never near Redwood Creek. One new rumor is that the cars have been moved to throw authorities off track. You and your friends may have stumbled upon the grinners actual hideout at Redwood Creek."

"Do the rangers believe my story?"

"You are the only survivor who can verify the existence of grinners. You walked out alive and confirmed the rangers' worst nightmare. One group of rangers was furious when the sheriff wouldn't let them interrogate you."

"Do you believe me?"

"I must believe something or I wouldn't be calling. Rumors also say the grinners only use knives on their victims. You may have seriously surprised them with your firearm. It's probably the only reason you're still alive." He chuckled. "Grinners must have counted on backpackers obeying park regulations."

"Who are the grinners?"

"There's not much evidence. Some rangers suspect remnants of the Charles Manson Family. They believe Redwood Creek is a secret training center for new recruits. The grinners teach the newbies total obedience to the Family as well as the Manson tactics of creepy crawling and skeletal stalking. During his trial, Manson told his family to 'go into the wilderness and wreak havoc.'"

"What about the grins?"

"They're to scare the hell out of outsiders. It certainly seems to have worked on you."

"I can't get those grins out of my mind."

He said, "Something else happened after you left. On a routine patrol, a ranger turned up missing in an area near Muir Grove. A wilderness corridor connects Muir Grove to Redwood Creek. It's only about four miles from your campsite. It's also an area where some abandoned trenches and bunkers were recently found. Park official are freaking out."

"They need to close the park."

"Listen to me, Lake," he said. "The main reason I'm calling is to warn you. Rumor has it those bastards are mobile and have a long reach. Most of them don't stay in the woods for very long. Your name and picture have been in the newspapers. It's been reported you live in Los Angeles. I found your address in the phone book. If I can locate you, so can the grinners."

"You think they're in L.A.?"

"I think your life may be in danger. If I were you, I'd move to a secluded spot and be careful who I tell."

"I don't have the money for that," I said. "If they're here, they're already watching me."

"Keep your powder dry, Lake," he said.

Chapter Twenty-Five

Saugus Railroad Station

Bud and I were assigned the unenviable task of bracing shipments of glass inside boxcars at the Saugus Railroad Station. It was a Thatcher Glass tradition that no one else could be on duty while the carpenters braced the boxcars. It was considered bad luck. People who work with glass tend to be very superstitious. Once the trucks and forklifts dropped off their loads, they left.

Bud had developed a system. I climbed into the boxcar and shouted measurements for the framing braces. He did all the sawing and nailing and then pushed the braces to me inside the car. I hung upside down and set the braces into position. Using a nail gun with a long hose, I finished the job.

The gig at the Saugus Railroad Station was our finest ruse. Bud had the other supervisor convinced it took at least one hour per car, when in actuality it was only twenty minutes. After we finished, we had forty minutes to rest or have a beer at the Saugus Bar across the highway. The bar opened at 7:00 a.m. and on weekend mornings had a lively trade. On weekdays, however, the place was dead.

Saugus was searing. It was already ninety-six degrees and no telling how hot inside the boxcars. Our first break came at 8:30 a.m. Mr. Saugus, the bartender, was the only person in the joint. No one knew his real name. He was bald, stocky and maybe fifty years old. He looked like a former Hells Angel and did not have a sense of humor.

Bud put salt and Tabasco sauce in his Coors. I took it naked. The beer tasted so good it weakened the knees. Unfortunately, the bar had no air conditioning and it was hotter inside than on the porch. The smell of sweat, piss and whiskey permeated the establishment.

I said, "There are no cars in the parking lot."

"So?"

"Where does Mr. Saugus park?"

"He probably lives under the bar."

We stood on the porch and watched the trucks return with another load of glass. Kerls drove the lead forklift.

He said, "We need to talk, Lake. My military friends want to meet you. They've got a plan."

Bud said, "Manny's tonight?"

"Not tonight," Kerls answered. "I'm working overtime."

I said, "Me neither. I'm taking Kendall to a party in Canoga Park."

Kerls shook his head. "I've no idea what that foxy girl sees in you."

Bud said, "She has a sweet ass."

"All right," I said, "enough about Kendall. How about Saturday night?"

"Saturday night is good."

Bud and I finished the next two boxcars. There were no people on the train or at the station. Maybe a car passed on the highway every ten minutes. It was getting hotter. We crossed the street to the Saugus Bar.

"I'm roasting in here," Bud said. "Let's sit on the porch."

It was 11:45 a.m. and we were working on our third beers. A car pulled into the parking lot, but no one got out. The car just sat there revving its engine. Bud and I watched. The windows were tinted and we couldn't tell if it was two girls or a gang of Martians.

I said, "They're beginning to get on my nerves."

"Screw them," Bud said. "They don't want to leave the air conditioning."

The car slowly backed out of the lot and pulled onto the highway. The next load arrived and we watched Kerls and the boys do their jobs.

Kerls said, "We're taking a long lunch. You can disappear until 2:00 p.m."

"We're getting a little smashed," Bud said, holding up his beer. "The heat ain't helping."

Kerls said, "You wanna white cross? Keep you running until dark."

"Sure."

When the crew left, Bud and I swallowed our white crosses with backwash and threw the cans onto the scrap pile. Just then a car pulled into the railroad station. Though it was a newer model, the windows were tinted just like the previous one. It sat in the empty lot with its engine revving.

Bud said, "What's wrong, Lake? You're as pale as a sheet."

I spilled the beans about the deputy's phone call and the supposed long reach of the grinners. I believe even Bud took notice.

He said, "You think grinners are in the car?"

"I've no idea."

"Let's find out."

Armed with framing hammers that were extra long with large waffle heads, we approached the car in a casual manner. Instantly, it zoomed out of the lot.

Bud looked at me. "Whoa," he said.

Chapter Twenty-Six

Canoga Park

The Canoga Park Ranch was a sprawling five-acre oasis with oaks, eucalyptus and horse corrals in the heart of a Valley ghetto. I despised Canoga Park. It was filthy and resembled a third world nation. The ranch, however, was like a piece of Santa Barbara.

I wasn't certain how many of my friends lived at the ranch, but there were plenty. It had a main house with at least five bedrooms. Several smaller structures had been converted into *casitas*, including a former chicken coop.

Driving south on Desoto in my truck, Kendall crossed Sherman Way. She made a right on Kittridge, and we saw at least one hundred cars parked on the street.

It was a good bet most of the partygoers knew Louis. He was the type of guy who knew everyone. I dreaded the possibility of questions about Redwood Creek, especially since many of those questions had begun to feel like interrogations.

Kendall said, "Relax. Tonight is gonna be fun."

"I just don't want to talk about Louis."

"People know that, Lake. No one wants to talk about a murder at a party."

For the most part, Kendall was correct. People were cool and seemed to genuinely encourage me to have a good time. Though the party covered the entire grounds, most of the action was around a bonfire in front of the main house. Someone at the ranch owned a superb sound system. Jimi Hendrix and the Doors seemed to be the main diet with a splash of Deep Purple and the Rolling Stones. There was an abundance of good booze and dope along with loads of stupid conversation and laughter. It was just what I needed.

"When's Louis getting here?" a guy named Jerry with piercing hazel eyes and a jagged scar on his left cheek asked.

I turned to face him. "What are you talking about, Jerry?"

He said, "C'mon, Lake. No body has been recovered. No one believes he's dead."

I said, "Have another beer."

"Is it true you never really saw what happened to Louis or Todd?"

Now I glared at him. "About a minute ago I was having a good time."

"Don't be like that, Lake."

Kendall came to the rescue. "Go away, you fucking jerkoff," she roared.

"I live here," Jerry responded.

"Then go to your room."

He stomped off, scowling.

I said, "Nice job, Jane Fonda."

"Don't let him annoy you."

"I won't. I'm having fun."

She said, "Let's go to the chicken coop. I heard people are doing tequila shots."

"Fine with me," I said. "I graduated from Monroe High School."

"So?"

"I was raised on tequila."

"A bit of the Valley wit, I see."

As we approached the converted chicken coop, two people spotted us and quickly went inside. Without a doubt, the chicken coop was the nicest remodeled building on the property. It had a great room with a high-beamed ceiling and wood floor. There was a kitchen, dining room, side bathroom and two bedrooms. Most of the people crowded around a table in the dining area. On the table were sliced limes, saltshakers and several bottles of Jose Cuervo. The ritual had already begun. First you wet the skin between the thumb and forefinger, and then sprinkle on a tad of salt. Then in one swift motion, you lick the salt, drain the shot and bite the lime. It was considered an art. People have modified the sequence in many creative ways. Obviously, the drunker the participant the more hilarious the sequence. Kendall and I took a turn.

She asked, "What did you mean you graduated from Monroe High School?"

"At Monroe," I said, "it was a tradition to sneak back onto the field after football games and drink shots of tequila. I believe the tradition continues to this day."

"We should walk over there on Friday night to see if that's true."

I said, "Where did kids from Van Nuys High School get drunk?"

She thought for a moment. "At the Van Nuys Drive-In or parking lot of Bob's Big Boy."

Someone yelled, "Group shot."

About twenty people bent over the table with their backs to us and took shots. After sucking on their limes, they turned toward me and grinned. Not a smile, mind you, but a full-throttled grin as described by the third article in the *L.A. Times*.

Not a word was uttered. I grabbed Kendall by the wrist and bolted for the door. Two people inadvertently blocked my path and were rudely shoved in the face. Others burst out laughing.

Someone yelled, "It was a joke, Lake. You should have seen your face."

"Didn't have to punch me," another said. "I think my nose is bleeding."

I was hyperventilating. I said, "I'm not sorry. You shouldn't be fucking with me."

"You were supposed to laugh, not go apeshit."

When we were alone, Kendall confessed, "I was in on it, Lake. I thought you'd think it was funny."

"Last week a deputy from Merced County called and warned me that the grinners could be in L.A. My name and picture have been in the *Times*. There's a chance I'm being stalked…so I don't think it's funny."

"I'm so sorry," she said, nearly in tears. "I believe you."

"You're in a small minority."

"What are you going to do, Lake?"

I shook my head. "Try to stay alive."

Chapter Twenty-Seven

Back to Manny's

I walked the four blocks down Sepulveda to Manny's with Kendall and waded through the sleaze. On the corner was a seedy strip joint with *The Classy Lady* in purple neon. To the south were a railroad overpass and two fleabag motels infested with prostitutes. In the shadows of the overpass, teenage drug addicts stuck needles in their arms while transvestite whores hit on unsuspecting johns looking for a good time.

The Dodgers were on KTTV. Ron Cey, also known as the Penguin, had just belted a three-run homer and waddled around the bases.

"You're getting paranoid, Lake," Kerls said, after I told him about the deputy's phone call and Saugus Railroad Station.

"No," Bud said. "I was at the railroad station. It may have been nothing, but it sure got my attention."

"There's more," I said, and told them both about the prank played on me in Canoga Park.

"What do you want to do?"

I looked Kerls in the eye and said, "I'm ready to go back."

"Fucking-A."

Kendall said, "No, you're not."

I turned to her. "I don't want to go back, but I can't live like this anymore. Do you understand?"

She said, "If you're going, I'm going with you."

"Like hell you are."

"I want to go. Let me make up for the Canoga Park prank."

I said, "It wasn't the prank that bothered me, it was my reaction to the prank. I don't blame you."

"Why can't I go?"

"Because the forest is full of fucking killers and I don't want anything to happen to you, Kendall. Kerls knows if it turns ugly it'll be every man for himself. I can't protect you."

Bud asked, "When do we leave?"

"You're not going either," I said. "I appreciate the offer and would love to accept, but you have a family."

"C'mon, Lake."

"You're out, Bud."

He sipped his beer. "Lemme know if you change your mind."

I looked at Kerls. "It's true what I told Kendall. If things turn out like they did with Louis and Todd, I don't know how I'll react."

"You'll be fine," Kerls said. "It's not going to be like last time. We expect them to fuck with us…but this time we'll be prepared."

"What's our next step, Kerls?"

He said, "We bring in Chris and Sara."

Chris had been in a rifle platoon in Vietnam, and Sara was apparently the tougher sibling. She had also served in the army. Their father had trained them both with firearms before puberty.

"How do you know them?"

Kerls said, "Chris has lived in my building for over a year. They're both obsessed with your story about grinners. They can't believe you're my friend."

"They don't even know me," I said. "Why would they risk their lives going to Redwood Creek?"

"Ask them yourself. They want to meet you."

"Why are you goin', Kerls? You're a good friend and I'm grateful for the support, but this could be really dangerous."

"I believe you," he said, simply.

"Why? Why do you believe me when practically everyone else thinks I'm full of crap?"

"You said it yourself, Lake. You're not this good of an actor. Plus, it's exciting."

"It might be terrifying."

"We'll be in good hands," he said.

Chapter Twenty-Eight

County Line Surfing Beach

The Valley was washed in blinding morning sunshine. I turned off the Ventura Freeway onto Las Virgenes Drive and entered Malibu Canyon. On the other side of the tunnel, where the painting of a nude pink lady reigned in glorious splendor, a thick fog bank had settled over the entire North Bay. The temperature dropped fifteen degrees.

Kendall and I were going surfing.

"My head hurts," she said.

"Poor girl."

"I'm never drinking again."

"Never?"

She smiled. "Never tequila."

A car with four surfboards strapped to the top was returning to the Valley. I stuck out my thumb. Almost immediately three thumbs pointed upward enthusiastically.

"Must be big," I said.

"I want to go with you to Redwood Creek."

"Absolutely not, Kendall."

She pretended to pout. "I think you're sweet on one of those grinner girls."

I glanced at her and winked. "I'll bring a dude home for you."

County Line surfing beach was situated on the Los Angeles-Ventura county line. I parked my truck on the shoulder of the Pacific Coast Highway. There was no beach or sand at County Line, only a cliff strewn with rocks. The water was as smooth as a black mirror with eight foot swells rolling in off the point.

Five or six surfers sat just beyond the breakers.

Kendall and I trod carefully down the rocks and found a flat spot to sit. Though it was summer, I still put on my full wet suit. I left Kendall sitting comfortably and posing like a *Sports Illustrated* swimsuit model.

"Look," she called out, pointing to a group of vans with the *Surfer Magazine* logo. Several photographers stood on the edge of the cliff with an arsenal of cameras. "It's your day to make *Surfer Magazine*."

I stood in knee-deep water and waxed my board. Then I rubbed a handful of sand into the coating. Several lines of four-foot high soup rumbled toward the rocks. Paddling out was going to be a challenge.

I caught my first eight-foot swell off the point and it closed out immediately. I barely got out alive. My second wave was perfection. Dropping in quickly, I banked off the lip and kicked up a gust of spray. Surfers paddling out hooted.

"The waves are fast," I said to two surfers at the take-off point.

"Getting bigger too," one said. "I think your wave topped nine feet."

"Lake," a voice screamed from shore.

I looked, but the fog was blocking out the rocks.

"Lake," the voice screamed again, only louder.

"Look at that," a surfer exclaimed.

A swimmer was heading in our direction, taking long strokes like the great Duke Kahanamoku. It was Kendall.

"Isn't that your girlfriend, Lake?" another surfer asked.

I said, "What the hell is she doing?"

I paddled toward her.

"Lake," she gasped.

I grabbed hold of her arm. "What are you doing, Kendall?"

She pulled herself up on the nose of the board. "Two girls sat next to me on the rocks," she said. "I didn't think anything about it until one of them whispered, 'Kendall.' It was so faint I wasn't sure I actually heard it. Then the other girl spoke louder. 'Kendall,' she said, 'don't say we didn't waaarrn you.' I looked to my left and they were both grinning. I mean, fucking satanic grinning. I leaped into the water."

I looked toward the rocks, but the fog still blocked my view.

Kendall said, "One of them was chunky."

"Chunky?"

"Well built, actually, and very muscular. I don't want to go to Redwood Creek now."

"Climb on the board before you freeze to death," I said. "I'll swim in the water."

"Hey, Lake?"

"What?"

"My head doesn't hurt anymore."

Chapter Twenty-Nine

289 High Performance Mustang

Norm was in the driveway working on his 1965 Mustang. It was a maroon 289 high performance coupe. I recognized the car instantly. Louis had driven it as a teenager.

"I love that car," I said, walking up the driveway.

Norm glanced at me and smiled. He knew I was thinking of Louis. "Most people who love Mustangs never seem to grow up."

"This one's a beauty."

The situation stung. I knew Norm had been fixing up the car before our Redwood Creek trip to surprise Louis.

He said, "What color was yours?"

"Dark green, like Steve McQueen's in *Bullitt*."

"But you had a '66. McQueen's was a '68."

"Mine wasn't a fastback either."

"What happened to her?"

"I blew the engine on that fucking paper route." I had delivered seven hundred papers every night for the *L.A. Times*. V8 didn't handle the stop-and-go stress very well.

"I remember."

"I cried for a week," I said.

Norm stopped working and looked at me. "What did you come here to tell me, Lake?"

I took a deep breath. "I'm going back to Redwood Creek next week. I have to find out what happened to Louis and Todd."

"I want to go with you," he said.

"No, Norm. If something happened to you, I'd never forgive myself."

"You can't do it alone."

I told him about our team and what little I knew about the plan. "This guy Chris is a Vietnam veteran and apparently knows his shit. It's going to be like a military operation."

Norm said, "Okay, you go back with a tough guy and big guns. What do you hope to accomplish?"

"I'm going to find Louis and Todd, or kill some grinners in the process."

Norm sat in the front seat of the Mustang. "I say I want to go, but that's a lie. I'm too old and scared for that kind of shit."

"I'm scared, too. That's why I have to go. I don't want to be scared anymore."

He said, "Don't get killed over this, son. It's not your obligation."

I drove my Ford pickup to O'Melveny Park at the end of Balboa. After hiking about a mile up Bee Canyon, I made a left and began to climb Mission Peak, the most prominent and recognizable foothill in the North Valley. I reached the summit in about an hour.

Near the top were four stunted oak trees. They provided the only shade. I sat under an oak and watched the jets fly in from Simi Valley and bank toward Van Nuys Airport.

As I sipped a Coors, I thought about Norm and Redwood Creek.

Chapter Thirty

Lake Calls Sparky

I dialed Sparky's number. I said, "You deserve to know about the operation. But first, I want to tell you about a short story I wrote last year."

"Okay," she said.

"One year ago, Louis, Todd and I were driving home after visiting a college buddy in Thousand Oaks. We thought it would be fun to take old Simi Pass rather than the 118 because it passed the Lone Ranger TV set and Spahn Ranch, the old hideout of the Charles Manson Family. After pulling up to the ranch, we got out of the truck and started goofing around. It was a real spooky place, but we were drunk and had liquid balls. When we were ready to leave, I stepped up to the gate to take a leak. Louis and Todd got into my truck and started the engine. While I was pissing, Louis eased the truck into gear and slowly pulled away, calling out, 'Give our regards to Charlie.' Suddenly, a semi truck barreled around the corner and nearly smashed the pickup. When I reached the door, Louis and Todd were hyperventilating."

"Todd told me about that," Sparky said. "Why are you telling me now?"

"In my story, I had the semi truck crash into the pickup and kill my two best friends while I stood next to the gate taking a leak. The driver of the semi was also killed. I was trapped at the Manson ranch. There was nothing I could to do and nowhere to go. I stood alone in the dark with the ghosts of my two friends for forty-five minutes until the first ambulance arrived. In the following days, I was forced to face you and Norm and attempt to explain how at least six lives were destroyed in one existential moment."

Sparky was breathing hard into the phone. "You wrote that before the trip to Redwood Creek?"

"Six months before."

"I just got the chills."

"Two weeks ago, my story became our reality. Instead of a semi truck, it was a band of knife-wielding crazies with grins. But please believe me, I'll never write a story about the grinners."

Sparky sighed. "Tell me about the operation, Lake."

"We're going back to Redwood Creek, armed to the teeth, to kick some grinner ass. I've got to find out what happened to Louis and Todd."

"I'm going with you," she said, firmly. "I made up my mind."

Chapter Thirty-One

The Team

The team huddled in a booth at Manny's bar. On KTTV, Steve Garvey of the Dodgers delivered a game winning walk-off single in the bottom of the tenth. Kerls made the introductions and everybody shook hands and nodded.

Chris appeared tough and his sister, Sara, even tougher. They both wore camouflage pants and black t-shirts with 9th Battalion Air Cavalry emblazoned on the front. Sara had long blonde hair and was pretty in a rugged way. We drank a shot of whiskey and washed it down with Coors Original draft.

Sara held up her glass and said, "To Redwood Creek."

"We'd better have our act together when we get there," I replied.

Chris issued his first command. "Me and Sara give the orders. And the number one rule on this operation is that everyone does exactly what we say. If anyone has a problem with that, speak up now."

We all shook our heads.

Chris turned to me. "I'm intrigued with your story, Lake. I hope you're telling the truth. I plan to go into Redwood Creek like it's the Ia Trang Valley in 'Nam."

Kerls nodded enthusiastically. "Fucking-A."

Chris said, "Are you on the level, Lake?"

"Yes, sir," I said staunchly.

"Prove it."

Sparky began to recite a list of missing people cited by the *Fresno Bee*.

Chris said, "No, I want him to prove it." He stared into my eyes. "Kerls told me you're a writer."

"That's true," I said. "But I could never write about shooting an old dude in the face and watching blood spurt out the back of his skull."

Chris nodded, approvingly. "Go on."

"I ran off while my best friend was being hacked to death. Now I'm living in a hellish nightmare. If you think I'm lying, drink up and walk away. Sparky, Kerls and I will go it alone."

Chris smiled. "Okay, then. We're a team. And if those grinners really exist, you're gonna need us."

"If you hardly believe my story, why are you willing to risk your life?"

"If your story is bogus, then there is no risk. If the story is true, then it's gonna be a fucking rush."

I said, "You don't care about Louis and Todd. You guys are mercenaries looking for kicks."

"That's one way to put it, but me and Sara are intrigued. If you're telling the truth, we're the ones you want giving the orders."

"You're just adrenaline junkies."

"Lake," Kerls snapped. "Chris is cool. I'd trust him with my life."

I looked at Sparky. "What do you think?"

She said, "I'm satisfied."

I nodded.

Chris said, "Okay, then. Now for the fun part. Sara and me have come up with a plan that includes plenty of badass military tactics. But remember, we give the orders. No discussion, no democracy."

The tattooed waitress brought us another pitcher of Coors.

Turning to Sparky, Chris said, "I hear you have a primo van. You'll haul the equipment and weapons. Lake will drive his four-by-four in case we need to haul our asses outta there quick."

"How's this thing going down, Chris?" I asked.

"We'll adapt to the situation. Basically we do military reconnaissance followed by ambush or assault, if needed. We locate Louis and Todd, and capture a grinner. If there's a situation, we kill every motherfucker in the woods. Or we have a pleasant camping trip. When we're in hostile territory, everyone needs to put on his or her fucking game face. We leave Thursday."

Sara stood up. "On Wednesday, we'll meet at the shooting range up Bouquet Canyon. Chris and I have some outrageous toys for you to play with."

"AR-15s," Chris said.

Sparky smiled. "I love target practice."

Part Three

The Return

Chapter Thirty-Two

On the Road Again

The team met in the back lot of my apartment building at 7:00 a.m. We loaded the equipment into the vehicles and prepared to take off. Among the various guns were four AR-15s with ten boxes of ammo. Sara and Sparky drove the van; Chris thought the girls should bond. He also wanted Sara to pick Sparky's brain about my character. Neither Chris nor Sara seemed entirely satisfied with my version of Redwood Creek.

The boys piled into the pickup.

Sara said, "We'll follow you."

Rather than taking the shortcut up Balboa to Old San Fernando Road and joining I-5 north of the San Fernando Valley, Kerls suggested taking the more direct route up Sepulveda and catching the 405 at Rinaldi.

I said, "We'll hit heavy traffic when the 405 merges with I-5."

Kerls said, "Not this early in the morning, dude. Trust me."

Chris said, "I think Lake is right, Kerls."

"Listen to me one time," Kerls said. "You're both such nonbelievers."

I shrugged and headed up Sepulveda. Within five minutes, we sat on the 405 in the type of traffic that causes mental disorders.

"Good one, Kerls," I said.

After an hour of crawling toward Valencia, we had traveled only six miles. Chris asked, "Is it too early for a beer?"

"Absolutely not," I answered, pulling off at Magic Mountain Parkway. The girls followed us to a 7-Eleven. Sara decided she couldn't drink a beer this early in the morning without a bag of boiled peanuts.

"There's a stand near the entrance to the amusement park," she said.

Kerls said, "What the fuck is a boiled peanut?"

Sara replied, "Just what it sounds like, dumbass. It's a raw peanut that's been boiled in salty water."

"Why would I want to eat that? Isn't the peanut squishy?"

Sara said, "I thought the same thing. I was repulsed when I first opened a wet shell and saw a mushy peanut, but after popping it into my mouth, I became an addict."

"Look what I found," I said, walking out of the 7-Eleven. "A dollar twenty-nine six-pack."

Sara grimaced. "There's no way I'm drinking a cheap-ass beer called Brew 102."

I said, "Didn't figure you for finicky."

"You may be repulsed at first," Kerls mimicked, "but when you open that first wet can and pour the Brew 102 into your mouth, you'll become an addict."

"No one likes a smart ass, Kerls," Sara said.

Chris rolled his eyes. "Shut up, both of you. We're not even out of L.A. County and you're driving me nuts."

Chapter Thirty-Three

A William Golding Novel

It was in plain sight the moment we drove into the remote trailhead parking lot.

I pointed. "That's the same forest maintenance truck I saw when I was here with Louis and Todd."

"What are you saying?" Chris asked. "The forest maintenance guys are grinners?"

I glanced at Chris. "It's peculiar, that's all."

We had driven all day to make the trailhead by evening. Chris decided to hike in using flashlights. He said it would be hard, but that no one would expect it and we'd have the element of surprise. His plan was to rest throughout the morning while setting up the perimeter and then begin military procedures in the afternoon.

I said, "What are those maintenance guys doing out here at this hour?"

Chris said, "Give it a rest."

"Why?"

"Because I still think you might be punking us," he said. "C'mon, Lake. What do Louis and Todd have planned for us?"

Sparky said, "What are you talking about?"

"Chris is only staying alert," Sara said. "Lake sounded too eager about the truck. I caught it too."

Chris said, "I like to keep all my options open."

"Well, keep this open," I said. "Fuck you."

"Don't take it personal. There could be one hell of a prank waiting for us out here."

"I suppose you loaded our clips with blanks."

"Okay, drop it. If I came on too strong, I apologize. I'm just trying to cover our asses."

At that moment, a station wagon pulled up with a family of backpackers. As they streamed out of the wagon, they couldn't help but notice our assault rifles. Mom, Dad and several teenagers abruptly halted their conversations and stared at us.

Chris didn't miss a beat. "A rogue bear attacked four hikers yesterday," he said in an officious tone. "We're going to tranquilize the animal and transport him to a less-populated area."

Mom asked, "Was anyone injured?"

"It wasn't pretty, ma'am. I'd check first with the rangers before camping out here." Needless to say, they left in a hurry.

The packs were heavy. Besides the usual gear, the guns and ammo weighed a ton. By the time we made it to the bridge, it was 10:00 p.m. and totally dark. Kerls and I listened to the creek and sipped Jack Daniel's from a flask.

Sparky said, "I got a bad feeling, Lake. Maybe this was a mistake."

I took hold of her wrist and offered some Jack Daniel's. "I ran off and left Todd. That won't happen to you."

I quickly found the first orange tin square. Our flashlights shone deep into the woods. As we inched forward, time began to drag.

After about a mile, Chris said, "This is an impressive hike, Lake. It's a tough bushwhack. How much farther?"

Coming from a guy who bushwhacked the jungles of Vietnam, it sounded like a compliment. "A mile, maybe."

He said, "How did you discover this trail?"

I told him about Louis's 1954 map.

Sparky said, "I feel like I'm in a William Golding novel."

"Seems more like Stephen King," Kerls said.

I looked at them both. "Don't either of you mention James Dickey."

Chris said, "How about a novel titled *Shut the Fuck Up?*"

Chapter Thirty-Four

Military Mindset

Sunrise on Redwood Creek. The twin waterfall made its usual roar. Chris went into his military mindset.

First we set up a perimeter using our gear and tents as boundaries. Our fire pit and safe zone were within the perimeter. Everything outside of it was considered hostile enemy territory. Chris ordered us not to venture outside the perimeter alone.

Next we set up our command post, which was Sara's tent backed up against a redwood. Extra ammo was kept inside the command post. Each of us was armed with at least two guns at all times. I carried an AR-15, my thirty-eight and a small thirty-two semi automatic. I kept the thirty-eight in a shoulder holster and the thirty-two in my back pocket.

It was time to rest. We had driven all day and hiked for much of the night. While two people guarded the perimeter, three others could sleep.

Chris pointed to a small rise. "That's a perfect location for the guards," he said. "Anything approaching the perimeter should be visible."

I nodded toward a slope opposite the guard hill. "They tied Louis to the first tree."

Sara said, "Chris and I aren't convinced Louis is dead."

When Chris saw the look on my face, he said, "Leave it alone for now, Sara."

"We may be able to use the slope to our advantage."

"I'll make a mental note, Lake," Chris said. "We'll begin offensive measures in the morning."

The f irst day passed quickly and without incident. By the time everyone was fully rested, it was late afternoon. Chris had fashioned a camouflaged guard station using rhododendrons piled in front of a large redwood next to his tent. He gathered us in front of the station and explained our first-night procedures.

"Me and Sara will go on a short reconnaissance before dinner. No one ventures outside the perimeter while we're gone. The hours for night guard duty are 10:00 p.m. to 6:00 a.m. Everyone rises at 6:00 a.m. You'll go in this order: Sara, Kerls, Sparky and Lake. I'll take the last shift. The guard will take cover in the guard station and lean against the redwood. I made a comfortable perch. Not even a fucking mosquito will be able to creep up behind you because of the tree. Stay awake and alert. If anything suspicious enters the perimeter, and I don't care if it's a horny porcupine, you fire off a shot. Your first priority is to warn us, not to fight off intruders. If we hear a warning shot, we storm out of our tents and massacre everything in sight. No campfire after dark. I don't want to attract attention or illuminate the perimeter. Cook with camp stoves and use flashlights only when necessary. While it's still light, however, we can enjoy a small blaze."

We all agreed the south side of camp would be the Land of Shat. Sara stuck a small army shovel in the dirt just before the tree line. No one was allowed to visit the Land of Shat alone. Chris was adamant. He claimed a person was most vulnerable when using the Land of Shat.

When Chris and Sara returned from their reconnaissance, there was a slight chill in the air. I was the acknowledged fire starter; even Chris and Sara deferred. There had been a hard rain the day before and it was difficult to find decent wood. I put forth my best effort. Using the driest twigs, I built a perfect tepee and placed the larger sticks close by in order to feed the flame. It was bittersweet when I used Todd's strategy of crawling under boulders for dry wood. I had saved our paper bags from the 7-Eleven and ordered everyone to collect all paper scraps. As I began to crumple the paper into a small pile, I felt something greasy on my fingertips. It smelled like dog shit.

"What's this?" Then I noticed skid marks on the paper. "Who put used toilet paper in the pile?"

Sara looked at me sheepishly. "Just trying to contribute. I thought all you extreme backpackers wasted not."

"You might have warned me," I said, looking at my hands. "Who has the fucking soap?"

Chapter Thirty-Five

Return of the Ranger

It was twilight when Sara sounded the alarm. In a nanosecond the camp bristled with deadly weapons. The intruder was immediately covered. Chris signaled to check our fire. We waited.

"Hello to camp," a familiar voice called out. "I'm coming in."

A ranger rode into camp on horseback. He looked us over and said, "You campers are breaking at least a dozen park regulations."

We lowered our guns.

I was doubly incredulous. "You," I said. "What are you doing back here?"

"Might ask you the same question."

I lost control. "You know damn well what I'm doing here, you motherfucker."

"Lake," Chris snarled. "Be respectful."

"He knows all about the grinners, Chris."

Kerls said, "I can't believe you're out here by yourself."

The ranger turned to Kerls and said, "I've ranged for twenty-two years by myself."

"This is bullshit," I said. "He pulled the same stunt when I was out here with Louis and Todd. Still looking for salamanders, you liar?"

"You look exactly like Keith Carradine," Sparky said.

I nodded. "Todd said the same thing."

"We saw him in the movie *Pretty Baby*."

"Lake has a point, mister," Chris said. "What are you doing out here?"

"He told us about the grinners," I said before he could answer. "He claimed they were squatters who refused to give up their land to the Feds or maybe remnants of the Manson Family."

"Charles Manson?" Sara exclaimed.

"I also told you I never saw a grinner."

"He knows Louis and Todd didn't run away."

Chris said, "Maybe you should explain yourself, mister. Are his friends dead?"

The ranger answered, "I don't know anything for certain. There have been several other disappearances."

"Why are you here?" I said.

"I spotted your vehicle. There haven't been any other backpackers in Redwood Creek for three weeks."

"Bullshit number two," I said. "We chased away a family at the trailhead yesterday. I suspect you let us enter Redwood Creek."

"Why would I do that?"

Kerls said, "This guy knows something. He's setting us up."

"Something is definitely going on," I said, "and he won't tell us."

"I agree, mister," Chris said. "Maybe you should start by being truthful."

The ranger looked down at his saddle horn. "You want it straight?"

"I think you owe it to us," Chris said.

"Two days after his incident," he said, nodding at me, "a ranger on patrol vanished in Muir Grove. We want to find out what happened to him without causing a panic."

Sparky said, "What about the missing Tucson girls?"

"They disappeared in this area too."

"So you're keeping out all backpackers?" I said.

"Yes."

"You would have turned away the family at the trailhead if we didn't run them off?"

"Yeah."

"Then why'd you let us come in?"

"Who said we let you?"

Even Sara wasn't buying it. She stood up and looked menacing. "Enough bullshit, dude. What's really going on?"

"You shouldn't have come back," he said bluntly, ignoring Sara. "It's too dangerous. You're way out of your league."

I said, "You going to report us?"

He smiled. "What for? No one would believe me except that sheriff from Merced County. He's been watching out for you, Lake."

"You know my name?"

"All the rangers in Kings Canyon know your name. You're a celebrity."

I said, "The sheriff isn't doing jack shit about what happened to my friends."

"What do you think you're going to accomplish?"

"We're going to stir things up."

He said, "You need to go home, Lake. You could all get killed."

Sara put her hands on her hips. "Don't worry about us," she said. "Turn your ass around and get the fuck outta here."

The ranger had not dismounted. He looked at me. "I'll come back in a day or two. See if you're still alive."

Chris shot the ranger a cold look. "You do that."

After he left in the same direction he had come, Kerls said, "I think Keith Carradine the ranger is a grinner."

"He could be a spy," I said. "The grinners attacked us not long after his visit."

Chris said, "I should have tagged him."

Chapter Thirty-Six

Night Talks

I served beef stew and whiskey for a late snack. Everyone took pride in bringing a signature dish for an evening meal, including a special brand of whiskey. We had Jim Beam, Jack Daniel's, Wild Turkey and Old Crow. Sparky brought several bottles of chardonnay. Our equipment was top of the line, and we argued over the merits of REI, L. L. Bean and North Face. The weapons proved impressive too. We had all smiled after the ranger took respectful note.

Before turning in for our first real night of sleep, Chris walked the perimeter and listened. Kerls started to speak, but Chris held up his hand.

"We'll wire the perimeter in the morning," he said. "Later, we'll carry out our first ambush outside of the safe zone."

Sara prepared to take the first watch. During our snack, we were treated to an incredible lightning and thunder show without rain. The flash and boom seemed to make everyone jumpy. It was the first time Sara appeared shaken.

"I'll take first watch," Kerls offered.

Sara eyed him with contempt. "Screw you, Kerls. I don't believe that creepy ranger. There are no grinners back here."

A few hours later, I climbed out of my sleeping bag to take a leak. A wall of darkness greeted me. I flicked on my flashlight to get my bearings. Kerls called out softly, "No lights, Lake."

Just then a bolt of lightning lit up the entire camp followed by a clap of thunder. I saw Kerls leaning out of the guard station with his semiautomatic rifle in hand. The image made me feel secure. When it was my turn for guard duty, I relieved Sparky and took up my position in the tiny guardroom. It was 2:30 a.m. I didn't feel safe any longer. I kept both pistols in hand and battled with anxiety.

At 4:00 a.m. Chris walked me to my tent. He said, "You need to understand I still have doubts about your story."

"I almost hope we don't find anything."

"Sara and I will finish the week, but with the exception of that weird-ass ranger, I've seen nothing out here to convince me of menace."

"Why do you think I agreed to come back?"

"I don't know, maybe to make your story sound more believable."

"My story?"

"Louis had gambling debts and Todd wanted to escape his marriage," Chris said. "You're covering for your friends in order to write a best-selling story about grinners."

"You sound like the Merced County sheriff."

"Sara believes Louis and Todd are hiding in the woods. She expects them to pull some tricks on us."

"Why?"

He said, "If we all believe there are grinners, you'll have your witnesses."

"That makes no sense. We could kill someone out here."

"We'll stay for the week and follow procedures. If nothing happens by the end of the week, I expect you to tell me the truth."

"Jesus, Chris."

He grabbed my arm. His grip was like a vise. "If something does goes wrong, Lake – no running this time."

Chapter Thirty-Seven

Reconnaissance and Ambush

At sunrise, Chris took charge and explained our first operation. "I discovered a primo locale for our first ambush," he said.

Across the creek f rom the hill where the grinners had tied up Louis there was a flat area. It had a clear view of the entire camp. The plan called for Sara and Sparky to have their morning coffee at that spot, and then leave an AR-15 rifle leaning against a tree. Chris set up two ambush sites that formed an outstanding crossfire.

Kerls had his doubts. "They won't fall for it."

"Who won't fall for it?" Sara asked. "I haven't seen any sign of another person or camp. This is bullshit."

"Great attitude, Sara," Sparky said.

"Shut up, Sparky," Chris ordered.

I said, "You shut up, Chris. We're following your lead, but Sara doesn't seem to be on board. We may as well go home if she's going to cop a fucking attitude."

"Shut the fuck up, Lake. I told you me and Sara are here for the duration."

"Then stop bickering," Kerls said. "We need to stick together."

Chris relaxed. "Put all the extra guns in Sparky's tent," he said. "It's closer to the guard station and easier to watch."

Chris, Sara and Sparky took the high position in the trees while Kerls and I hunkered down by the creek. Ambushes really sucked. They were incredibly stressful and boring. If any action occurred, I was certain it would be incredibly frightening.

After five hours of a well-executed ambush, only a raccoon had sniffed the rifle. Chris pulled the plug.

Sara said, "That was a waste."

"Don't push it, Sara," Kerls answered.

"Why not?" Chris said. "She's right."

Sara went into a martial arts stance. "Try me, Kerls. I'll knock you on your ass."

Sparky pulled me aside. "What are we doing out here, Lake? They don't believe us."

"We stick out the week."

"Please. Have you been truthful with me?"

"Yes, Sparky. I don't know what else to say."

Back at camp, things got uglier. I felt compelled to defend myself.

I said, "Louis and Todd were murdered. None of you were there so don't tell me it's bullshit. I'm the only one who's seen a grinner and survived. We can leave right now if that's what the group decides."

Chris said, "I told you no democracy."

"Boo-hoo, Lake," Sara said.

Sparky said, "Why don't you both shove off. You may be good soldiers, but your hearts aren't with the mission."

For a tense moment it was silent.

Kerls approached the group. "I'm with Sparky and Lake. That ranger convinced me something weird is going on. Sparky's right. You two need to split."

I nodded. "You're bringing us down."

Kerls held up his flask of Wild Turkey. "To Louis and Todd," he said, before taking a big slug. Sparky and I took our turns, but didn't pass the flask to Chris or Sara.

"To Louis and Todd," Sparky said.

I felt the warmth from the Wild Turkey. "Go home, Chris," I said. "You can take my truck."

Chris rose to the occasion. He said, "I apologize, Lake. Things may not add up, but Sara and I will conduct an attitude change."

I looked at Sara. "I didn't hear her say it."

Sara stared at the ground. "Okay, I'm saying it now."

I handed her the whiskey and smiled. "You realize we were bluffing," I said. "We'd be scared shitless out here without you guys."

In the late afternoon, Chris and Sara went on another reconnaissance. They wanted to go alone in order to incorporate their special military tracking. Kerls, Sparky and I were not amused. Without the pros, we felt admittedly vulnerable.

After sunset, Chris and Sara returned. "You'd think I'd find at least a candy wrapper," Chris said. "Those grinners are neat sons of bitches."

I lit the fire and began to set up for dinner. The twin waterfall continued to roar. In two minutes, Chris stormed from his tent and exploded with rage.

"Not funny, you fuckers," he bellowed.

Sara was equally furious. "Who did it?" she demanded.

"Did what?" Kerls asked.

"You know what."

"We should pull out in the morning, Chris," Sara said, seething with rage.

I stepped forward. "What's wrong?"

Chris said, "Have you been in camp the entire time we were gone?"

"Yeah."

Sparky said, "Except…"

"Except what?"

"We went down to the creek to filter water."

"All of you?"

"Of course."

"Motherfuckers," Chris roared. "You broke the number one rule. You left the perimeter unguarded."

"You still haven't told us what's wrong."

"All my gear is in Sara's tent and her gear in mine."

"Someone switched up our tents," Sara said. "The extra ammo is missing too."

We stared at one another.

Chris laid out five items on the ground. They were carvings of faces with demonic grins. "This was in my tent," he said. "One for each of us."

"Holy shit," Kerls cried.

I picked up one of the carvings and cut my finger on a jagged tooth again. "Goddamn it."

"Who is fucking with us?" Chris shouted.

Chapter Thirty-Eight

Rough Night

That night there was an unusual amount of birds chirping. The first two nights had been relatively quiet. There appeared to be a pattern to the chirps.

Sparky scanned the perimeter. "If those are birds, their intelligence level has jumped up the evolutionary scale."

Chris said, "If those are humans, they're damn fucking good."

"It's only birds, you dumbasses," Sara said.

"Just before Todd saw a grinning girl," I said, "he heard birds chirping."

Then the crunching in the woods began. It was across the creek and a long way off, but slightly disconcerting because of the weight and volume.

"What the hell is that?" Kerls asked nervously.

"Wildlife," Sara said, this time not so convincingly. "Chris and I saw a bear. It smells our food."

We climbed into our tents and the bizarre noises continued. I couldn't sleep. During Sparky's watch, missiles began to fly into camp. A few hit my tent. It was breezy, so I assured myself the wind was merely blowing around pinecones and other debris. When it was my turn for guard duty, I found Sparky on edge.

"They've been aiming at me," she said.

"Who has?"

"Whoever is out there."

I stared into the woods. "It's breezy tonight."

"It's not the wind, Lake. I was bombarded."

"It's okay now."

"Listen."

The crunching in the woods started up again. Now it seemed much closer.

"I feel like screaming," Sparky said.

For a brief moment, I thought I saw tiny lights. I looked at Sparky. "Fireflies?"

"Or candles."

"I'm going to pop off a few rounds," I said.

"Don't," she said. "Chris will be furious."

In the morning, Sparky's mental outlook had not improved.

"I want to go home, Lake," she said. "I'm terrified."

Everyone gathered at the fire pit for coffee. "It was birds, wind and a bear," I said, with absolutely no certainty.

"I was hit by rocks."

"Bullshit," Sara said. "Twigs hit my tent all night. Rocks would have caused damage." Turning to me, she said, "I told you we shouldn't have brought her."

"Shut up, Sara."

Chris said, "You shut up, Lake."

"She's out of line, Chris."

"Yeah, I know."

I tilted my head. "You know?"

"While I was on guard duty, rocks rained down on me too."

Sara said, "Chris, it was only the wind."

"Wind doesn't throw rocks, Sara."

"What are you saying?"

He cocked his semi automatic pistol. "I'm saying someone is still out there fucking with us."

Kerls said, "It's that cocksucker ranger."

"Perhaps," Chris said. "But it's more than one person. Those rocks were coming in from different angles."

Sara said, "It's Louis and Todd."

"That is so fucking stupid," I said. "If Louis and Todd were throwing rocks at us, they might get shot. I almost fired a few rounds at those tiny lights."

"Tiny lights?" Chris said.

"Sparky and I saw tiny lights. They may have been fireflies or candles."

Sara thought for a moment. "Kerls is right. It's Keith Carradine the ranger and his buddies." Glaring at me, she said, "I guaran-damn-tee you're mixed up with them."

I said, "Why would you associate me with the ranger?"

"Simple, Lake," Chris said. "You know each other."

Chapter Thirty-Nine

Kerls

We ate our breakfast of oatmeal, granola bars and coffee. The forest was conspicuously silent, no chirping or flying missiles. There wasn't any more loud crashing on the perimeter.

Everyone was glum.

Chris was lost in thought for a while. Then he smiled. "I got an idea," he said. "We use Sparky as bait."

"Why Sparky?" I asked.

"It's obvious they targeted her. They must have a good reason."

Chris claimed if we made it look like the four of us went on a reconnaissance, while leaving Sparky to guard the camp, it would seem natural. He had discovered two excellent routes in the underbrush for us to sneak back just outside the perimeter and set up our ambush. This time Kerls and I would take the high ground. The genius of the plan was that Sparky wouldn't just sit in one spot looking like a setup. She would patrol the perimeter and perform usual tasks. Our rifles could cover every position in camp.

I shook my head. "No, Chris. It's too dangerous. Our number one rule is to never be alone and now you want to break the rule when things turn dicey?"

"What dicey?" Sara said. "Nothing has really happened."

Chris said, "She won't be alone. We'll have her covered at all times."

"It won't work," Kerls said. "They didn't fall for the rifle."

"The rifle just sat there," Chris said. "It was too obvious. Sparky will be walking around camp and provide them with plenty of opportunity."

I said, "I still don't like it."

"I'll choreograph her every move so she'll look natural and we'll know exactly where she's supposed to be at all times."

Sara said, "Let me do it."

"No, don't you see? Last night, for some reason, they targeted Sparky. Maybe they recognized her picture in the papers and know she's Todd's wife."

Sparky was scared, but intrigued with Chris' plan. "So what if I'm Todd's wife?" she asked.

"They may figure you're the most vulnerable," Chris responded.

I said, "They must've seen my picture too. I killed their old dude and they'll want revenge. I should be the bait."

"They'd be more cautious with you because you have killed," Chris said. "They picked on Sparky last night."

Sara said, "If they've been watching us and think Sparky is our weakest l ink, they may get careless."

This was the first real time Chris and Sara seemed to believe we were in danger.

Kerls said, "I'm with Lake. It's far too risky."

Sparky suddenly blurted out, "I'll do it." We all turned to look at her. "It may be our best chance."

Chris really knew his shit. The operation was textbook. Kerls and I went out a quarter of a mile, then hit the brush and crawled back. Chris and Sara waited by the creek for ten minutes and then took off on their route. By that time, Kerls and I were in position and covering Sparky. I never saw Chris and Sara return, but I knew they were at their site. Sparky played her role flawlessly.

After nearly four hours, Kerls turned to me and said, "They're not coming."

Once again, Chris pulled the plug.

Everyone was exhausted from lying in wait and lack of sleep. I sat next to the fire pit and stared at the ground.

Sara said, "Good time for lunch and a nap."

I said, "I want to coffee up."

"Me too," Kerls said. He meandered down to the creek to filter water.

Chris tapped my shoulder and motioned for me to follow. We belly-crawled to an embankment overlooking Redwood Creek and watched Kerls. I looked at Chris and he put two fingers against his lips.

At the creek, Kerls filled the coffee pot and a gallon water jug. Because of the mission, it was easy to overlook that we were camped in the largest redwood forest in the world. The Giant Forest in Sequoia had bigger trees but Redwood Creek had the numbers. Despite the circumstances, the area was hauntingly beautiful.

Kerls glanced up creek and seemed to admire the thick groves of redwoods. He approached the nearest grove and patted the trunk of the first tree. It shot straight up and poked a hole in the sky. Then he noticed a red tank top lying on the bank of the creek. It was about fifty feet away. When he was ten feet from the tank top, he spied a girl in the creek washing her hair. She was topless.

"Whoa, excuse me," he said. "I didn't mean to sneak up on you."

The girl turned toward him with her breasts fully exposed. "Hello. Did you see my two friends?" she asked nonchalantly.

"No, I didn't."

"We're on a day hike and I wandered away from them." She waded out of the water and picked up her top without putting it on. "Where'd you come from?"

Chris and I got a good look at her. She was pretty in a natural sort of way.

Kerls said, "I'm camping a little farther down the creek."

"My sandals," she said. "On the rock. Could you hand them to me?"

"Sure," Kerls said.

When he bent down to pick up the sandals, she lunged at him with a long glistening blade in her hand. He looked up and saw her hideous, demonic grin.

Two shots were fired in such quick succession that they seemed like one. Both slugs slapped the girl in the center of her naked back and she flopped face down on the rocks. She didn't move. Kerls looked at her and dropped the sandals. Chris was standing on a rock on the other side of the creek with his AR-15 still smoking. I stood behind him.

"Did you see her grin?" I asked nervously. "We saw her knife but not the grin."

Kerls was shaken. "Fucking-A I saw her grin. It was the scariest shit I've ever seen."

Chris looked at me. "Lake, you have your witness."

Chapter Forty

Final Ambush

She was dead all right. A gob of blood spattered the rock. She had two gaping holes on each side of her body. Her eyes were wide open. Naturally, Chris had a plan.

"Someone clean her up," he said, "and haul her ass up to that hill where they tied Louis. We'll sit her up against a tree and make it look like she's reading a book. With any luck, we can nail a few more of those grinning bastards."

"I'll do it," I volunteered. "I don't mind the blood anymore."

Chris looked at me and shook his head. "Lake, I sincerely apologize. I can't imagine what you went through with Louis and Todd."

"Let's hope you don't find out."

"You have to admit your story was insane," Sara said, picking up the dead girl's long blade.

I nodded. "Welcome to the jungle."

She said, "I'm sorry for doubting you."

Sparky approached the group. "I don't know what to say, Lake."

"Nothing…it's not necessary."

I saw the tears and took Sparky into my arms. Chris, Sara and Kerls joined us in a group hug. "I know Todd is gone now," she said.

"I never doubted you, Lake," Kerls said. "Bud swore you're too dumb to make up such a yarn."

I said, "We may be in serious trouble."

"No way," Chris said. "We have those grinning fucks on their heels."

We ate rice and coffee'd up. Chris helped me wash the girl's body. Sparky gave us a t-shirt to cover the bullet holes. We placed her on the hill against the same redwood where the fiends had tied Louis, and propped up a book on her lap. Kerls and I hunkered down next to the creek while the others took the high ground. From my vantage point the girl appeared to be alive and reading.

After about ten minutes, rocks started to fly into the camp perimeter. They hit the center of the fire pit and began to walk like mortar rounds toward Kerls and me. Scores of them rained from the sky, closer and closer, until they finally infiltrated our position.

Kerls said, "Those motherfuckers." We covered our heads and retreated to the command post.

Chris yelled, "Shoot back. They're firing at you."

"Shoot back? Where?"

Sparky took control. By the angles of the rocks, she quickly calculated their origin and shouted instructions. We opened fire with extreme prejudice. It was our first all-out firefight and we turned the woods into a free fire zone. At least seventy rounds ripped into the trees. Smoke hung in the air. The rocks finally ceased.

Sara made a startling discovery. "The body is missing."

We all looked at the hill. During the shooting, the girl's body had vanished.

I said, "We have our proof. Let's pull out now."

"What for?"

"The attack is coming any moment."

"It's better strategy to fortify the high ground and let them come to us," Chris said. "They started it. We'll finish it."

Chapter Forty-One

The Horror

It started at twilight.

As we chewed beef jerky and sipped coffee laced with Old Crow, there was a flurry of activity on the hill where the body had disappeared. We took up defensive positions and briefly spotted several grinners scurrying about in the shadows. Then we saw what they had done.

The bodies of Louis and Todd, well over three weeks deceased, were tied to the tree. They were bound together at the neck. Though there was serious decomposition, it was definitely Louis and Todd.

"Those sick fucks," I wailed.

Sparky's hands clamped firmly over her mouth. Chris wisely blocked her view and sat her on the ground.

"Stay strong," he advised. "It's a psychological ploy. The VC pulled the same stunt with American bodies in Vietnam."

I said, "We're all dead."

Chris shook my arm. "Lake," he hissed. "Keep it together."

Sara and Kerls fired a burst into the trees. I joined them.

"I want to kill them all," Sara said.

"We'll pull out at first light," Chris said, visibly shaken.

"No," I said. "We pull out right now."

"There won't be enough light for a pullout."

"Chris," Sara said. "I agree with Lake,"

"They're coming," I said. "I know it."

Chris wrinkled his brow. "Okay," he said. "Let's break camp and assume our positions. Do it now."

We started to break camp and it must have been the moment the grinners were anticipating. Bird chirps sounded from nearly every direction. Rocks began to bombard us again. The chirps and rocks appeared to be pushing us toward the corridor of the lost trail. It seemed obvious that the grinners had something special planned.

I said, "They want us to take the lost trail. Maybe we should follow the creek."

"The terrain is too difficult for our retreat strategy," Chris said. "Everyone follow procedures."

I looked at Sparky. "Can you make it?"

She nodded, still trembling.

"Saddle up," Chris said. "Lock and load."

"What about the equipment?"

"Fuck it."

The chirps and rocks had ceased.

Chapter Forty-Two

Retreat

Chris and Sara dropped to one knee and prepared to cover our retreat. Kerls, Sparky and I raced toward the first orange tin square. The rock throwing was ferocious. At one point we heard voices and then shrieks. I got nailed in the cheek by a rock and spit out a tooth. Kerls grabbed my arm to steady my knees.

We stopped at thirty yards, dropped to a knee and signaled to Chris and Sara. The plan was to repeat the procedure all the way to the loop trail and then set up an ambush using the bridge as cover.

During our next maneuver, gunshots rang out. Chris and Sara returned fire. Kerls was struck in the shoulder and a splat of blood sprayed across my face. Before I could get down on one knee, a dozen grinners flanked our position and waved their deadly long knives. The attack was swift and savage. Chris and Sara took the brunt. Both were hit by bullets, Chris seriously. A score of gleaming blades sliced into their arms and legs.

"They've been overrun," I said, my voice sounding surreal. I was frozen with fear.

Sparky said, "Help them. We need to join the fight."

We rallied. Kerls led the counterattack by swinging his rifle like Davey Crockett at the Alamo.

Pulling my thirty-two semi automatic, I opened fire and charged. Kerls was knocked to the ground and swatted at the knives with the stock of his gun. Several of my shots were point blank into arms and torsos. Sparky remained at the orange tin square and fired her AR-15.

It started to rain. A grinner fell upon me swinging two blades. I peered deeply into her eyes and recognized one of the two chunks from the Redwood Creek trailhead. This was a delicious moment. I took careful aim and put a bullet into her neck. She fell flat on her back and started to choke. I knelt down and pointed my gun at her face. Raindrops washed the blood from her wound into a small stream. She tried to speak.

"Yeah, I know," I said. "You got to expect rain in the Sierras."

I pulled the trigger.

Sara and Kerls had been cut countless times. Their arms, shoulders and hands dripped with bright red blood. Chris was curled up in the dirt, bloodstained and no longer in the fight. Sara held her ground and rapidly fired her nine-millimeter pistol.

"Collect all the ammo," Sara said. "We make our stand here."

Suddenly, two sugar pines creaked above our heads and then crashed to the ground in spectacular fashion, cutting off our only escape route.

Sara shouted, "Pick up Chris and place him under those trees."

The grinners hit us with brute force. As Kerls and Sparky dragged Chris, they were assaulted from the rear and stabbed in the back. All three tumbled to the ground. Sara and I had to toughen up. We stood back to back and fired bursts from the reloaded AR-15s, but it didn't seem to be enough.

Our situation appeared bleak, especially when I spotted another group creeping up behind us under the toppled sugar pines. Somehow they had managed to circle around and cut off our retreat.

We're fucked, I thought.

"Hit the ground," a familiar voice shouted. I looked closer and saw Keith Carradine the ranger with about twenty armed companions. They had large FBI letters on their jackets. Agents braced machine guns on the sugar pines and laid down a lethal spray. Other agents rushed past us and stormed into the redwoods.

I tripped over Chris and fell on my ass. He had four bullet holes in his back and agents were applying pressure to his wounds. Automatic fire continued in the distance, but for us the battle was over.

Chapter Forty-Three

ℱℬ𝓘

The ranger offered a hand and pulled me to my feet. He said, "Let me introduce myself. I'm agent Rob Burgess, FBI."

I shook my head in disbelief. "Nice of you to show up."

"Sorry about the disguise. I've been undercover for two months."

I pointed to Chris. "He's hurt real bad. He saved our lives."

"We have a chopper on the way."

FBI medics swarmed around us. Cotton pads soaked up the blood and IVs were connected. We received the royal treatment. Chris was critical. He had three gunshot wounds to the stomach and one in the upper chest.

Sara asked, "Is he going to be okay?" She had been winged in both arms.

"He's in excellent hands," Burgess said. "All of you will be airlifted to Fresno Memorial."

I said, "I thought you were a grinner."

"We thought *you* were a grinner."

"Why?"

"Your old map looked phony. Even veteran rangers didn't know about this trail. Apparently it's older than King Canyon National Park."

"We followed it by the orange tin squares."

"The disappearance of your two friends was puzzling. If you were grinners, why fake a disappearance? Some agents believed you were setting up a trap. But when you returned with a new group, I figured your story was authentic."

"But there are other disappearances," I said.

"Most were local cases that had plausible explanations, until two months ago."

I nodded. "The Tucson girls."

"It was the Arizona legislature that requested the FBI."

"Must be nice to have influence."

"If the majority of the other cases involve grinners, we may have twenty to thirty victims."

"What is that old maintenance truck at the trailhead?"

"High-tech headquarters. Remember the four backpackers you startled on your first trip? They're FBI agents."

Two agents approached and conferred with Burgess. It continued to sprinkle. Sparky and Kerls were still getting patched. The rock that hit me in the face had actually knocked out two teeth.

Burgess said, "Twenty-two confirmed dead and eight in custody." He looked at Sara with admiration. "That was some fancy shooting, sweetheart."

Sara put her hands on her hips. "Call me sweetheart again and I'll knock you on your ass."

"Who are the grinners?" Kerls asked.

Burgess shook his head. "It's still a big mystery. Maybe we'll get more information from the suspects. We've traced elements of the grinners from Los Angeles to Santa Cruz, but there is no hard evidence linking them to Charles Manson."

"When did you start monitoring us?"

"An agent spotted your pickup truck at the entrance station. The bureau went into code red hoping you'd make contact. Park maintenance dug a lookout position for us about a quarter of a mile up a slope. You were under surveillance twenty-four hours a day. No agent observed a grinner until this afternoon."

I said, "So we weren't in quite as much danger as we thought?"

"Oh, no," Burgess said bluntly. "You were in extreme danger. It was your choice. You put yourselves out here and the bureau only took advantage. We'd pull you out if possible, but our number one priority was to locate the Tucson girls."

"Any word on them?"

"Not yet."

I looked at Chris. There was too much blood. In the distance, I heard a helicopter.

Acknowledgements

I wish to thank Chris Kent, Bobby Kent, Lawrence G. Larson, William C. Abbey, Howard Conrad, Louis P. Morrison, Rob Burgess and Todd Carstenn for their support, friendship and master camping skills.

Backpacking is Nirvana.

Thank you to Daniel Barth for his guidance and literary expertise. Every serious writer needs a Daniel Barth.

Special thanks to my editor, Gary Greenfield, for his insight and professionalism. Working with you almost had me believing we were back at the Van Nuys Drive-In chasing Dawn and Debbie.

About the Author

G. Kent lives in the wilds of the Ocala National Forest in North Florida. He was born and raised in Los Angeles. He is also the author of a novel, *Bandits on the Rim* (Tenacity Press, 2012), and *Running with Razors and Soul: A Handbook for Competitive Runners* (Bandit Press, 2013). For more information contact kentib@earthlink.net.

Back cover photo by Elaine Springer Kent.